Ever After

Truth or

Hair

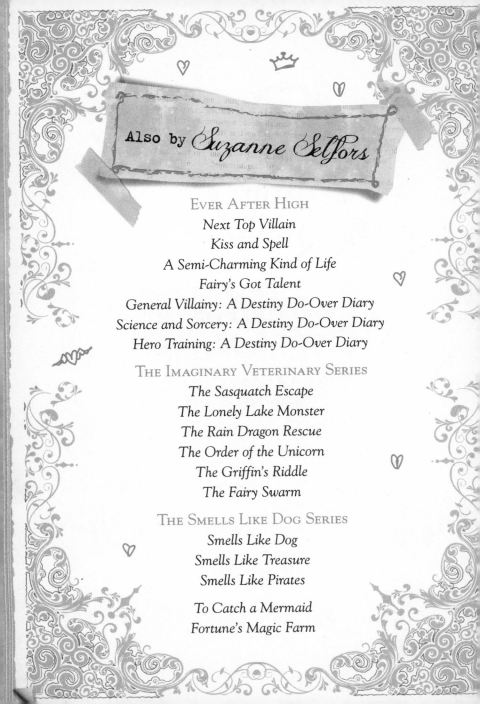

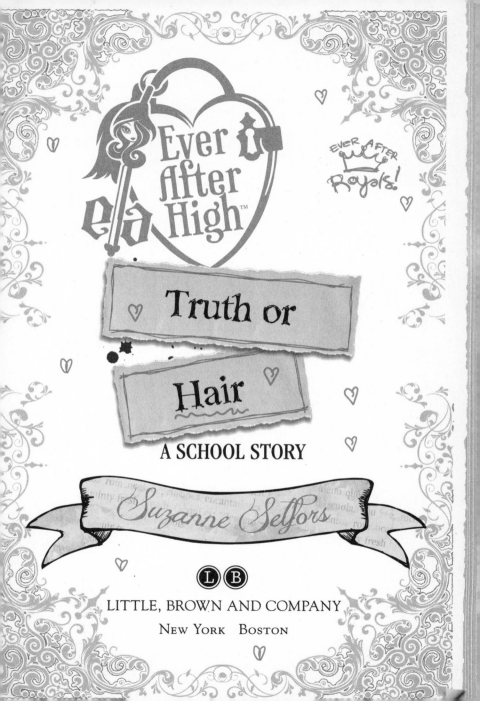

# Ever After High™

EVER AFTER Royals!

## Truth or Hair

### A SCHOOL STORY

Suzanne Selfors

**(L)(B)**

LITTLE, BROWN AND COMPANY

New York  Boston

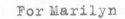

For Marilyn

Copyright © 2016 by Mattel, Inc.

Little, Brown and Company
Hachette Book Group
1290 Avenue of the Americas, New York, NY 10104
Visit us at lb-kids.com

Little, Brown and Company is a division of Hachette Book Group, Inc. The Little, Brown name and logo are trademarks of Hachette Book Group, Inc.

The publisher is not responsible for websites (or their content) that are not owned by the publisher.

First Edition: May 2016

Library of Congress Control Number: 2016931770

ISBN 978-0-316-40142-5

10 9 8 7 6 5 4 3 2 1

RRD-C

Printed in the United States of America

# Contents

# Bookish in Book End

According to the latest edition of *Flying Carpet's Travel Guide*, Ever After High was considered to be the most picturesque school in all the fairytale kingdoms—a majestic place, built from ancient stones and graced with decorative gardens and sparkling ponds. But even though most of the students considered it a home away from home, they enjoyed leaving campus now and then to escape the pressures of schoolwork and the ever-watchful eye of the headmaster, Milton Grimm. The nearby village of Book

End was often their first choice for a getaway—just a hop, skip, and jump over the troll-guarded footbridge and down the tree-lined path.

Book End harkened to a time gone by, with its thatched roofs, gingerbread exteriors, and cobbled lanes. But modern conveniences could be found there as well, with shops selling magically powered tech gadgets, pop-up boutiques carrying the latest fashion accessories, and baristas steaming milk for whatever beverage happened to be trending that day. In the same blink of an eye, a visitor might see curious things, like a teapot flying down the street, or a knight in shining armor shopping for shoes. The Beanstalk Bakery, the Mad Hatter of Wonderland's Tea & Hat Shoppe, and the Hocus Latte Café were all popular places where students liked to hang out. On most days, the village bustled with activity.

Holly O'Hair, daughter of the famously tressed Rapunzel, stood in front of her favorite Book End store, Yarns and Noble. Her wavy auburn hair tumbled down her shoulders and back like a cape. She stood, pressed up against a window, her green eyes nearly doubling in size, for she'd just made a happy discovery. The window display featured the latest book by Holly's favorite writer, Shannon Tale. The novel was the long-awaited conclusion to Ms. Tale's Princess Trilogy. It was Holly's hope that one day she'd publish a book of her own and it would be featured in the Yarns and Noble window. After writing hundreds of stories, Holly had narrowed it down to her favorite twelve, the perfect number for a collection. She already knew the title. *Tower Tales* by Holly O'Hair. She'd often dream of having a special event at a bookstore, where she'd give a little speech and then she'd read a few pages. Family and friends would attend. Shoppers would stand in line, waiting for her to sign books, just as she'd done so many times for other writers. What a great day that would be.

Her MirrorPhone chimed, waking her from the daydream. "Dearie!" The voice bellowing from the speaker belonged to a woman named Edith Broomswood. And the greenish face staring into the screen also belonged to Edith Broomswood. Once a member of the witch community, Ms. Broomswood had traded in her potions and pointed hats to become a high-powered literary agent to the stars. "Is this Holly O'Hair?"

"Yes," Holly said. She gulped. She'd sent her twelve stories to Ms. Broomswood five weeks ago. In order to get her story collection published and then sold in a store like Yarns and Noble, she first needed to secure a literary agent. Holly had been fastidious with her research. Ms. Broomswood came highly recommended. And she represented many bestselling authors, including Shannon Tale, so she had to be good.

"Dearie, I just finished reading your stories, and I'm feeling like a toadstool in the rain."

Holly had to think about that metaphor for a moment. "Does that mean you *like* them?"

"Like them?" Ms. Broomswood replied with a snort. She held the phone so close to her face, Holly could see right up her very long nose. "I adore them!

They are the bee's knees, dearie. The butterfly's thighs!"

A shiver of excitement darted up Holly's spine. Since sending her stories to Ms. Broomswood's office, she'd obsessively checked her messages for a reply. Would the famous agent want to help Holly get published? Until now, there'd been not a single word from Ms. Broomswood. The waiting had been agonizing. Holly had longed to hear anything. Even if it was a big rejection, at least she'd have an answer.

"I must have you as my client," Edith Broomswood said. She was walking and talking at the same time, so the phone was moving up and down. Holly caught a glimpse of a gleaming office tower, then a brief-case, then Ms. Broomswood's nose again. "I want to sell your stories to a publisher and make you rich and famous!"

Being rich and famous wasn't Holly's goal in life. But being published, well, that was her dream. Last year, she'd created a blog called *Fairytale Fangirl*. Every month, she took a well-known fairytale and gave it the Holly O'Hair twist—meaning she changed an element or two, thus turning it into a brand-new story. Writing was her favorite thing ever after. Having spent most of her life towerschooled, putting her stories *out there* had been scary. But all the positive feedback in her blog's comments section had helped build her confidence. She was starting to feel like an actual writer. And now this phone call was the biggest surprise of all. Could this really be happening? Could Ms. Broomswood sell her story collection to a publisher? Holly leaned against the bookstore's exterior wall as dizzy excitement washed over her.

Ms. Broomswood was still talking and walking. "First, however, you must sign a contract of agreement with me, allowing me to represent you as your literary agent." A piece of paper appeared on the MirrorPhone screen. "No need to read it, dearie. It's the same contract I use for all my clients."

"Even Shannon Tale?"

"Hexactly!"

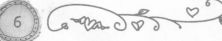

This was good news indeed. Holly signed with a trembling finger. The contract disappeared, and Ms. Broomswood's face filled the screen again. "Hexcellent! I'll call as soon as I get you a deal." Ms. Broomswood bonked the screen with her pointed chin. "Make sure you have your phone at all times!"

"Yes, of course," Holly said. "I won't let it out of my sight." She held back tears of joy. "Ms. Broomswood, how long do you think it will take?"

"There's no way of knowing. And there are no guarantees. While I think your stories are scrumptious, not everyone likes the classics. Ready yourself for failure—that's what I tell all my clients. If you're going to be struck by a lightning bolt of rejection, it's best to be standing firmly on the ground of reality than to be floating on a cloud of daydreams when it hits." She cackled.

That sounded like good, practical advice. But daydreaming was another one of Holly's favorite activities. "Thank you," Holly said.

"Broomswood out!" The call ended.

Just to make sure she wasn't daydreaming, Holly pinched herself. A sharp pain shot up her hand. Yep, this was real. She looked longingly into the bookstore window. If all went well, one day her book, *Tower Tales*, would be on display.

Her MirrorPhone chimed again. This time it was an alarm alerting her that she was running late for her appointment. She smiled. Not only had she gotten an amazing phone call, but she was about to see her favorite person in the whole world.

What a spelltacular morning this was turning out to be!

# A Sparrow

## on the Stairs

fter pushing her long hair behind her shoulders, Holly started across the road, carefully avoiding the ruts and holes where cobblestones had come loose. Her destination was the stone tower that stood in the center of Book End. It was tall, as towers tend to be, and topped with turrets. It housed three businesses, as evidenced by the sign in the tower's lobby, but Holly was only interested in one of them: the one in Suite C.

Suite A: MR. POP AND MR. WEASEL,
MULBERRY PURVEYORS
Suite B: DIDDLE DIDDLE FIDDLE REPAIR
Suite C: TOWER HAIR SALON

Holly stepped into the lobby. She'd been there so many times she'd lost count. Her destination on this visit, as on all previous visits, was suite C, which happened to be on the topmost floor. She didn't mind the steep climb. Ascending towers was a skill that had been bred into her DNA. Whether starting her education at home in a tower, visiting her mother's historic tower, or adjourning to her current tower dormitory room, it was always one step after the other, after the other. Ironic, however, that she'd been born with a fear of heights. It wasn't a paralyzing fear, but more of an annoyance that she'd learned to deal with. The best way to keep the fear at bay was to not look out the windows during the trek, for that would surely rattle her nerves. Instead, she focused on her feet and hummed. *Too bad stair climbing isn't an official school sport*, she mused to herself as the staircase wound upward. She was so excited about the mirror call from Ms. Broomswood, she hummed extra loudly.

You're getting closer!

This particular staircase was built of stone. Each stair had a slight dip in the center, worn down by generations of students who'd walked that very path to the salon, in need of a trim or perhaps a totally new look. The Tower Hair Salon had witnessed every style—fairyhive, porridge-bowl cut, and pixie perm, to name a few. The trek was steep and narrow. The stained-glass windows cast beams of yellow, pink, and blue, lighting the way. A few steps ahead, Holly's lion cub, Clipper, bounded here and there as he chased a spider. Holly had just picked him up from the Creature Day Care Center, and he was full of energy as usual. His ears alert, his rump wiggling

with excitement, Clipper prepared to pounce. But the spider found a crevice in the nick of time and disappeared. The cub growled with frustration. "Better luck next time," Holly told him.

*Don't give up—you're almost there!*

Holly smiled. She recognized the handwriting. It was so like her twin sister, Poppy, to provide inspirational notes. Poppy worked at the Tower Hair Salon as a stylist. Even though many of her clients found the hike tiring, they were willing to break a sweat in order to get their hair done by the most popular stylist in Book End. Holly laughed to herself. *Stairs are much better than having to climb a rope ladder woven from hair*, she thought. Which was exactly what her future prince was supposed to do. But her prince, whoever he might be, could rest assured that when the time came, even if he was decked out in armor, Holly's braid would be able to support his weight.

Under her mother's guidance, Holly had practiced braiding her luxurious locks with a technique that Rapunzel had trademarked. The resulting braid would provide perfect footholds for the prince's climb. "Don't worry," Rapunzel had told Holly when she was seven years old. "I've made improvements. If you follow my braiding technique, there will be barely any tugging on your scalp. It won't be painful for you, my darling."

Poppy had been watching the braiding lesson. "Why doesn't the prince use a ladder?" she'd asked. It was a perfectly logical question. "We've got lots of ladders out in the orchard. I climbed one yesterday to look at a beehive."

"Climbing a ladder is not part of the story," Rapunzel had explained.

Poppy had bit her lip, which was something she did when deep in thought. "Well, if he can't use a ladder, there are lots of other ways he could get into the tower. Why doesn't he fly on a Pegasus? Or get a magic carpet? Or, I know, why doesn't he just take the stairs? Huh? Why does he have to climb Holly's hair? That's so weird."

Holly waited for the reply because she'd wondered the exact same thing. Rapunzel pulled Poppy onto her lap and gave her a big hug. "I love your curious spirit," she'd told her other daughter. "I suppose that the prince could use those other means, if he chooses. It is not up to Holly *how* she gets rescued, but she will offer her hair, for that is how the story goes."

There were some who didn't understand such a tradition. Some believed that being destined for rescue was an old-fashioned storyline. Many of Ever After High's current students were mapping out their own stories, taking bold steps into unknown territory. This trend was a constant topic of discussion. But the truth was, Holly didn't see it as "old-fashioned." She was destined to be part of a classic love story, and that was an honor. Besides, her destiny wasn't stifling her life in any way. As a member of the cheerhexing team, as secretary of the Royal Student Council, and as an aspiring writer, she was honing many skills and living a well-rounded life. Even though having the fastest-growing hair in all the kingdoms was her trademark, there was a lot more to her than that.

"Whoa!" a voice called.

Sparrow Hood, son of the notoriously sticky-fingered Robin Hood, barreled down the stairs. He'd also been humming to himself, and he'd been moving so quickly, there'd been no time to stop. He tripped over Clipper and momentarily lost his balance. And began to fall…

"Oh no!" Holly cried. Without even thinking about it, she reached out and grabbed Sparrow before he could tumble down the steep staircase. Arms flailing, Sparrow almost knocked Holly over as he tried to find his footing on a narrow step. But somehow Holly managed to stay upright, even when Sparrow grasped her elbows and heavily leaned on her.

That had been a *very* close call. Speaking of close, the studs in Sparrow's leather vest were poking her arm. "Um, I think you're stable now. Would you mind letting go of me?"

"Oh right. No problemo." He smiled in a devilish way. Holly frowned. Was he at least going to say thank you to her for saving him? It wasn't that she *disliked* Sparrow; it was just that he was, well, different from most of the boys she'd grown up with. Firstly, he wasn't a royal. Secondly, he didn't partake in royal activities, such as Pegasus polo and coronation ceremonies. Thirdly, his destiny was to *steal* from royalty, as his father had before him. Fourthly, everything about him, from his studded boots to his music to his soul patch, was rebellious.

He was, in every sense, the bad boy on campus. And, in Holly's humble opinion, he tried way too hard to maintain that reputation.

They stared at each other. As her frown deepened, Sparrow finally started to pull away, but his leather wrist cuff got tangled in a lock of Holly's hair. "Don't pull," she told him. "Let me do it." She was an expert at untangling. Most days included

some sort of hair incident—someone tripping on her tresses, or sitting on them, or being momentarily blinded by them during a wind gust. Windy days were Holly's least favorite days because leaves would get stuck in her locks and it would take forever after to pick them out.

"This would make an awesome song," Sparrow mused as he watched her untangle. Then he started singing, "GIRL! *Your hair is all over my FACE! Why does it take up so much SPACE?*"

"Excuse me?" Holly started to point out to Sparrow that her hair was "all over his face" because she had just saved him from tumbling down the stairs. But then she thought better of it. She took a deep breath and straightened her tiara. She didn't feel upset with Sparrow. How could she? After such an amazing phone call from Ms. Broomswood, nothing could darken her mood. Besides, Sparrow was probably just embarrassed about tripping in front of her. "I think maybe Clipper got in your way and that's why you tripped. Sorry about that!"

"Yeah, that's definitely what happened. You should keep him on a leash."

"I've tried, but he always chews through them. Besides, it goes against his nature to be on a leash."

Sparrow shrugged. "Guess we cats gotta roam free." He reached over his shoulder, grabbed his guitar, which had been hanging against his back, and played a chord. *"FREE!"* he sang off-key. "Hey, whatcha gonna do when he turns into a full-grown lion?"

"Oh, that will never happen. Clipper is charmed. He'll always be a cub." She smiled politely. "Well, I need to…" She tried to step around Sparrow, but the space was too narrow.

"Hey, you should totally hear my new song. I'm gonna debut it at my upcoming concert." Sparrow had an indie rock band called Sparrow and the Merry Men. They did the occasional gig here and there, but this would be their first big concert. Thus far, ticket sales had been moderate. Sparrow's music wasn't everyone's favorite. Actually, he wasn't any-one's favorite, as far as Holly could tell, but the concert was a fund-raiser, so buying tickets meant supporting a good cause.

"I really don't have time. I'm already late for my appointment," Holly started to explain, but then Sparrow struck some screechy chords. They reverberated down the staircase. "GIRL!" he sang. "*You rock my fairytale WORLD!*" More chords. "*You make my brain stem SWIRL!*" The echo was so strong, Holly's teeth began to vibrate. "*You...*" He stopped singing. "I'm still trying to work out the rhyme."

"Uh, that was really..." So many great adjectives popped into her head—piercing, raucous, unpleasant. "Interesting. It was really interesting," she said finally. Sparrow winked. "Anyway, nice chatting with you but I'm late." Holly knew enough about Sparrow to know that he would stand there all day, singing, if she let him. He lived and breathed his music. Such passion was admirable, but his style of music wasn't exactly her cup of tea. She was more traditional in her tastes. A romantic ballad, accented by a lute and mandolin, was always appealing. "If you'll excuse me," she said politely, "I have an appointment with my sister."

"Hey, total coinkydink. Your sister just cut my hair. What do you think?" He posed as if modeling for a fashion shoot. "I think it rocks." He was clearly going for that "I just woke up and I don't care" look. Poppy had added some product to his hair to make it even messier.

"It's very nice," Holly said. "But I really need to get going. I don't want to keep my sister waiting."

"Sure thang." Sparrow pressed his back to the stone wall, his guitar raised above his head, and she squeezed past him. But after only a few steps, he called up to her, "Catch you later, *Holly O'Hair.*"

The way he'd said her name, with a little ring to it, made her wonder. Did he like her? *No, that's silly,* she told herself. Sparrow was a songwriter and a singer. Everything he said had a ring to it. She turned around. Why was he smiling at her in that weird way?

"Unfurl," she told him.

"Huh?"

"Unfurl rhymes with girl, and swirl."

"Oh, dude, that's perfect." He was still smiling. Then a guitar ringtone filled the air. He pulled a MirrorPhone from his pocket and read the screen. "It's one of the Merry Men. Gotta get this. Later, Princess!" He shot her another wink, then hurried down the stairs.

Oh no. He wasn't developing a crush, was he? Sparrow was not her cup of tea, and she wouldn't want to hurt his feelings.

But even so, she did appreciate Sparrow's artistic side. Though his words fit into a 4:4 rhythm and seemed to be about one thing, he was a fellow writer, and that was admirable. It took courage to write, but it took additional courage to send those words out into the world. Whether a song or a blog story, it was nerve-racking to wait for the audience's response. Would they applaud or boo? Would they download the songs or ignore them? Would they give the stories smiley-face or frowny-face emoticons?

Would they think the stories were good enough
for a book?

*Yay, you're here!*

Clipper was waiting on the top step, his head
cocked as if wondering, "What took you so long?"

She knelt beside him and patted his head. "Listen,
little one, please be good in there. It's not a jungle
for leaping and climbing. It's a salon, and there are
many things that can tip over." He nuzzled her hand.
Then he batted at her hair. That's when she noticed
a small plastic item that had gotten tangled in one
of her locks. It was a guitar pick.

It was definitely time for a trim!

The best person to handle her mass of hair was
her twin sister, Poppy. And Holly couldn't wait one
second longer to tell her the morning's news.

# Tower

# Hair Salon

Clipper bounded into the salon, Holly close behind. The salon's waiting room was decorated with an overstuffed purple sofa, framed mirrors, and a sleek chrome desk, which held the gold-foiled appointment book. The glass coffee table was covered in spellebrity news and style magazines like *Royal Life*, *Fairytale Fashion Week*, and *Troll Times*. The windows were open, allowing a gentle breeze to cut through the thick scent of hair products. There were shampoos for shimmer, sprays for volume, and gels that glued styles into place. Whatever adjective a customer sought—fluffy, sleek, smooth, or wild—there was a product to help achieve that result.

"Hi, sis," Poppy said, hurrying over to hug Holly.

"Hi," Holly said, returning the hug. Her sister's hair smelled like tangerine zest, a main ingredient in Poppy's favorite shampoo. Clipper wound around Poppy's legs, nuzzling against her and purring. She reached down and scratched between his ears.

An outside observer might not notice that the sisters were identical twins. While Holly wore her auburn hair long and flowing, Poppy's was trimmed in a short, asymmetrical style and dyed purple. The sisters' clothing choices were also very different. Holly tended to wear soft colors and classic styles, while Poppy loved bold colors like black and silver, and her clothes always had an edgy, modern vibe. Because she secretly decided to follow her own destiny and to not become the next Rapunzel, she didn't have to *look* like the next Rapunzel. So, over the years, she'd tried many different looks with her

hair. Poppy loved using her hair to express her individuality, and her current short purple do really suited her.

The girls looked at each other. Poppy smiled. "My twintuition's telling me that you have something to spill."

"And my twintuition's telling me that *you've* got something to spill," Holly said.

"It's true," Poppy said. "But it'll have to wait." She cocked her head, indicating the man who was standing over by the reception desk. "Sales call. I'll be done in a few minutes."

"Okay," Holly told her. But it was going to be difficult keeping her good news to herself. She wanted to open a window and shout it to the world!

As Holly settled onto the sofa, Poppy returned her attention to the salesman who'd stopped by the salon to pitch his products. He was a dapper fellow, dressed in a yellow suit, striped waistcoat, and long pointed shoes. His green hair stood straight up, like a perfectly mowed lawn.

"This is our latest," he was saying. He held a bottle in his hand, presenting it to Poppy as if presenting a newborn. "Curl Tamer. Guaranteed to hold those unruly curls in place."

"Some curls are super stubborn. How can you make such a guarantee?" Poppy asked.

"Observe," he said. He opened the bottle and spritzed the air. A little voice shot out of the bottle. "Stay!" the voice ordered.

Poppy laughed. "Let me see that." Bottle in hand, Poppy walked over to Holly. "Can I try this on you?"

"Sure," Holly said. Poppy aimed the bottle above Holly's right temple, where a small strand of hair curled next to her ear. It was the only strand on Holly's entire head that was wild and did exactly what it wanted. It had been creating chaos since birth. Holly usually tucked it behind her ear, out of sight.

Poppy spritzed. "Stay!" the bottle hollered. When Poppy stepped away, the curl obeyed.

"Does that bottle work on lions?" Holly asked as she tried to grab Clipper, who'd been sharpening his claws on the side of the sofa. "Clipper, stay! Stay!" He bounded between her feet, then around the salesman. When Holly finally scooped the cub into her arms, they both tumbled onto the sofa, Holly laughing, Clipper purring.

The salesman took another bottle from his satchel. "Of course, every once in a while, you will encounter a curl that isn't obedient, and that's when we recommend our Ultimate Curl Tamer." When he opened the bottle, the sound of a whip filled the air. Clipper wiggled out of Holly's arms and growled at the salesman.

"I guess he doesn't like that sound," Holly said.

"Yeah, I don't think I need that particular product," Poppy told the salesman. "But I'll try the first one." She bought two bottles of Curl Tamer and set them on the shelf. The salesman thanked her, then left. "We'd better get started," she told Holly. "We're running a bit late."

"I know, I'm sorry. I ran into Sparrow," Holly explained. "He started singing."

"Well, I guess singing is better than picking someone's pocket. But wait! What's your news?"

"Okay, I guess I'll go first." Once Holly started telling her sister her news, the words came out so fast, they all strung together. "Ms.Broomswoodcalledshewantsmeasaclientshe'sgoingtotrytosellmystoriestoapublisherImightgetpublished!"

Poppy squealed with glee. They both started jumping up and down. Then they hugged again. Holly gasped for breath. "So, what's *your* news?"

"I'm going to be the stylist for Sparrow's concert. I know it's just small-town stuff, but it'll look great on my résumé and it'll really strengthen my portfolio. And I get to show my work at a *real* concert." Holly squealed this time. The jumping up and down sent the coffee table wobbling. Once they'd calmed down, Poppy handed Holly a smock to wear over her dress. As Holly pulled it over her head, Poppy's smile turned into a look of puzzlement. "That's odd," she said.

"What's odd?" Holly asked.

Poppy pointed to Holly's feet. "Your hair isn't as long as it usually is on Monday."

"Huh?" Holly looked down. It was a well-known fact that Rapunzel hair grew faster than normal hair. Both girls had inherited this magical trait. Every Monday, Holly came to the salon with hair that was skimming the floor and had it trimmed so that it fell to her waist. By the next Monday, it would be skimming the floor again. But today, it only reached mid-shin. Holly had been so caught up in waiting for Edith Broomswood's call, she hadn't noticed. "I wonder why it's not as long."

"Are you sick?" Poppy asked, twirling a strand of her sister's hair between her fingers and looking at it closely.

"No, I feel fine." Holly's voice trembled a little when she said it. Perhaps all the fretting about the literary agent had stunted her hair growth. That made sense. Emotions affected everything. And even though she knew that worrying about her hair wasn't going to help, she started worrying more. Was something wrong with her *famous* hair?

"It's nothing to fret about," Poppy assured her, placing a comforting hand on her shoulder. "It's just a fluke. These things happen."

"Yes," Holly said with a brave smile. "It's a fluke." This day had been going so well; she wasn't going to let herself get all tied up in knots over a fluke, especially if her sister, the hair expert, told her not to be concerned. So she brushed the worry away.

Holly followed Poppy into one of the salon's styling rooms, which was warm and bright. The far wall was lined with four styling stations and four mirrors. Clipper found a sunny spot beneath a window. He stretched, yawned, then curled into a ball. With his tail wrapped over his nose, he took a catnap.

"Hi, Holly." Apple White, daughter of Snow White, one of the best-known fairytale characters of all time, was seated at the second styling station.

"Hi, Apple."

"So?" Her blue eyes twinkled. "Are you going to tell me why you two were making all that noise?"

Holly hesitated for a moment—after all, there was still a very real possibility that her dream might not come true. But she was in such a good mood, she couldn't hold back from sharing her news. "I might get published."

"Oh, that's spelltacular!" Apple said. "You deserve to be published. I just finished reading your new story. It was amazing. I was glued to my seat."

This compliment was an unexpected delight. No matter how much Holly liked her own stories, uploading the story to her blog was always a scary moment. Everyone had opinions, and these days, everyone expressed those opinions. So no matter how many nice comments Holly received on her blog, not everyone loved her work, and that was the reality of being a writer. But Apple's comment was extra important because, in this case, Apple wasn't just another reader. The most recent story Holly had written, titled "Snow Day," was based on Apple's mother, Snow White.

"You...*liked* it?"

"Well, of course I liked it," Apple said. "I especially liked the twist. Instead of hiding from an evil stepmother, Snow is hiding from an evil stepfather. It's nice to have some gender equality in the bad stepparent category. And instead of a little cottage in the forest, Snow hides in a ski chalet where the seven dwarves work as ski instructors. So adorable!"

"I told you people would like it," Poppy said warmly. "Writing is what you're meant to do."

"I sure hope so," Holly said. "And think of all the stories I can write while I'm waiting in the tower. It won't get in the way of my destiny."

Apple nodded. Like two peas in a pod, or two peas under a mattress, Apple and Holly were very much of the same frame of mind when it came to their royal duties.

"It's so nice that you both have good news," Apple said. "Holly might get published, and Poppy is going to style Sparrow and the Merry Men for their concert. What an enchanting morning."

Holly set her tiara onto the counter. "What's that?" She pointed at a little white ball of fluff that was floating around Apple's head.

"It's the latest drying technique," Poppy explained. "The cloud blows a gentle breeze, which results in a very natural look."

"Isn't it adorable?" Apple reached up and patted it. "And it doesn't make me feel one bit gloomy, even though it's a cloud."

"The upside is that it's nice and quiet," Poppy said. "The downside is that it takes a bit longer than the standard blow-dryer."

"I don't mind the hextra time," Apple said. "I'm using it to catch up on my reading." Her MirrorPad rested in her lap.

"I'm just glad you're not still using dragon breath to dry hair," Holly said. "That was way too hot. And it smelled kinda rotten."

"Agreed," Poppy said with a giggle.

Holly sat in a chair at the washing station, then tilted back to rest her head in a washing bowl. The bowl had been ordered from a specialty catalog for giants so that it would fit all of Holly's hair. While Holly closed her eyes and relaxed, Poppy shampooed, conditioned, then conditioned again. Music from the Red Shoes dance studio drifted in through the window. Holly's thoughts flitted between the phone conversation with Edith Broomswood and a future visit to Yarns and Noble where she'd be the featured author.

Poppy rinsed, then wrapped a giant fluffy towel around Holly's head. This had been their Monday-morning routine since Poppy had graduated from Sir Stuart's School of Beauty at the age of ten, the youngest ever to complete the certificate. Holly took her seat at the first styling station, next to Apple, who was reading something on her Mirror-Pad. After the shampoo and conditioning, the next step was the secret-formula detangler. Poppy bought the stuff in bulk, for it took two entire bottles to thoroughly coat all of Holly's hair. Poppy was gentle with the comb, unlike their childhood nursemaids who used to yank and tug with frustration. Holly remembered one morning when she'd run downstairs in tears, dozens of broken combs stuck in her hair as if she'd been caught in a comb tornado.

"Oh, you poor little dear," Rapunzel had said. "I think it's time to introduce you to my favorite product." She took Holly and Poppy to her private bathroom and showed them a bottle. Its label had been removed. "This is my little secret. This product is made specifically for Pegasus tails, but it's the best thing I've ever found for detangling my hair."

As Poppy worked the Pegasus detangler through Holly's hair, Apple looked up from her MirrorPad. "Poppy, I've always wondered, how did you know you were meant to style hair?"

"Oh, that's a really good story," Holly said.

Poppy grabbed a pair of trimming shears. "Since Holly is the storyteller, I'll let her tell you. That way, I can focus on my work."

"I'd be happy to tell it." Holly smiled. Sitting very still so her sister could trim with perfect precision,

Holly folded her hands in her lap. "It all began on the day of our birth. Of course, I don't remember being born, nor do I remember Poppy being born, but I've gathered information about that day, and about our early years, from reliable sources." And she began the tale.

## Chapter 4

# Shear Terror

Our mother, Queen Rapunzel, welcomed us into the world on a lovely spring morning. Songbirds twittered the news, as did the royal publicist. The air around the castle filled with hope, the trees outside the queen's window rustled with anticipation, and everyone bowed their heads, waiting for the heir's arrival.

My arrival.

When I was born, the first thing I did was look into my father's brown eyes, then into my mother's green eyes. My parents cooed at me and kissed my forehead. I stretched my little legs and yawned. Then I was swaddled in a pink blanket and carried into the grand ballroom, where relatives, friends, and villagers had gathered. As Father held me high above his head, applause filled the room. The O'Hairs had an heir to the throne, and all was well in the kingdom.

But then, just as Father was about to address the crowd and formally introduce me, someone shouted. Commotion arose. The royal physician rushed past, followed by nurses and attendants. I was quickly handed to Nanny Nona, the royal nanny. But even though there was so much chaos, I didn't cry out. It was nice and warm in that blanket, and I happily fell asleep.

The "commotion" was another baby, an unexpected surprise. "It's a girl!" the doctor exclaimed. "An identical twin!"

Just like me, Poppy looked into our father's eyes, then into our mother's. She yawned, stretched, and made a gurgling sound. Father was thrilled. Mother was blissfully happy. Another round of applause filled the air. Another pink blanket was sent for, and Poppy was swaddled. Feeling warm and safe, she, too, fell asleep.

"Ladies and gentlemen, friends and family," our father said, "today is the happiest day of my life, for Queen Rapunzel and I have been blessed with not one but with two daughters. Two!" He laughed, then slapped the royal physician on the back. "Seems some things can't always be predicted." The physician blushed.

Poppy was handed to Nanny Nona, who balanced us in her arms. "Smile," the royal butler said as he took a picture. Nanny Nona was so stunned by the morning's events, she could barely smile. She carried us into the nursery, where we were bathed and diapered. We were dressed in white gowns and tucked next to our mother. A golden crown was placed on my head, since I was the heir, and a silver crown was placed on Poppy's head. Then the first official royal portrait was taken.

"Two princesses?" Nanny Nona fretted. She tucked a stray gray hair into her bun, then smoothed her high-collared blouse and her long wool skirt. "How am I going to manage? I shall require assistance."

And so a gaggle of nursemaids were hired—white geese who'd been trained to change diapers, make beds, clean up messes, and, most important, to guard us while we slept. Like Nanny Nona, the geese were picky creatures who liked everything in its place. They also made excellent two-legged alarm systems.

As the days passed, I proved to be a happy baby and very easy to please. Whether watching sunspots swirl on a wall or butterflies flittering overhead, I was content to observe. I was also a huge fan of napping, which made me very popular with the nurse-maids, who also liked to nap.

Poppy also proved to be a happy baby; however, she was always on the move. She was the first to roll over, the first to sit up, and the first to crawl. "There she goes again!" Nanny Nona would cry at least three dozen times a day. The nursemaids would waddle as fast as they could, trying to keep Poppy out of harm's way. There were many near accidents as Poppy scooted too close to staircases, climbed into drawers, and tunneled under drapes. The royal carpenter was summoned. He set to work baby-proofing the entire castle. Gates were placed at the entrance to staircases, drawer and window locks were installed— all sorts of contraptions to keep the secondborn twin safe from her own curiosity.

So the story goes that one afternoon I was sitting on Father's lap, watching Poppy take her first steps.

"Don't you think it's odd, my dearest, that Poppy was born second?" Father asked Mother.

"Whatever do you mean?" Mother replied. She held out her hands, and Poppy stumbled toward her.

"Well," Father said, "Poppy has so much energy, one would think she'd have insisted on being born first." He chuckled.

"Holly was born first for a reason, my love. Poppy is not suited for waiting in a tower. She's too restless. Fairytale magic chose Holly."

"Yes, I guess that's true." Father hugged me. "Fairytale magic is wise indeed."

As we grew, though we remained different in demeanor, in appearance we were identical. Well, except for one little thing. While we'd each inherited our mother's famous auburn hair, which grew faster and thicker than "normal" hair, I had a single wild lock of hair, just above my right ear. It refused to drape, and it often stuck up and had to be pinned down. It was, in fact, the only wild trait I possessed.

Our hair had to be cut weekly, lest we trip over our own locks. I took the routine in stride. Even before I'd learned to read, I'd bring a picture book for distraction. That's when I began to fall in love with fairytales. Though it was often uncomfortable having my locks tugged and pulled as the tangles were combed out, I distracted myself with those wonderful stories, enduring the routine with royal resolve. But Poppy hated it. And she had no interest in my books. Why should she? She wasn't destined to live one of those stories, so she felt no need to read them. The nursemaids had to chase her, and it took at least three of them to hold her down. "It's like battling a wild baby yeti!" Nanny Nona exclaimed.

"Why can't I do it myself?" Poppy asked.

"Because you are not allowed to use shears," Nanny Nona said. "Now stop squirming."

Poppy squirmed harder. Shears snipped and clipped. Geese honked. Hair flew everywhere. As soon as the deed was done, Poppy made a mad dash for the door. She wasn't being bad or disrespectful. She simply didn't like sitting still and doing nothing. While my hair ribbons were clipped into place, Poppy's ribbons fell to the ground as she beat a path to freedom.

Being twins, we spent most every minute of the day and night together. Like most twins, we soon developed a sort of twintuition—the uncanny ability to sense what the other was thinking and feeling. And we worked as a team, on nearly everything. Which included teasing Nanny Nona. Though we loved her fairy much, we also loved tricking her. For, even though Nanny had known us both since the moment of our birth, she often couldn't tell us apart, especially if I tucked my wild hair behind my ear or covered it with a hat.

"I'm not Holly!" Poppy would holler as she tossed a book aside.

"And I'm not Poppy!" I would exclaim after bouncing on the bed. "We fooled you." We'd collapse in a heap of giggles. Pretending to be the other sister was one of our favorite things to do.

Nanny wasn't the only one who could be fooled. If we put on matching clothes and hats, we looked so much alike that even our parents fell for the trickery. Poppy, carrying a fairytale book in front of her face, would walk very slowly to the table and sit. "Hello, Holly," Mother would say.

"Hello, Mother."

Then I would run in and jump onto a chair. "Poppy, sit down!" Father would command. "I'd like to eat one meal without you spilling your milk."

We'd squeal with laughter. "My love, I think we've been fooled again," Mother would say.

And such was our childhood, filled with happiness and carefree days. But while I knew my storybook destiny, Poppy, being the secondborn, did not have one. What would become of her was a question on everyone's mind, especially hers. We began to realize, as a family, that Poppy's restlessness wasn't simply nature; it was fueled by uncertainty—the not knowing her destiny.

One night, at dinner, while waiting for the soup to be served, Poppy had something very important on her mind. "Father, Nanny Nona won't let me cut my own hair. She won't let me have a pair of shears."

"Nanny Nona is wise," Father said as he waited for the butler to butter his bread. "Shears are sharp."

"But I want to do it myself."

"That is not necessary. We have servants to do that."

"But—"

"But?" Father raised a disapproving eyebrow. Poppy closed her mouth and, with a loud "humph," sank low in her chair.

For Poppy, the shears became a treasure, of sorts, and when Nanny's back was turned, she'd reach out and try to grab them. "Poppy!" Nanny Nona cried. She pried the shears from Poppy's little hand. "Those are too dangerous. How many times must I tell you? You will cut yourself!" It became a battle of wills, with Poppy trying to outsmart Nanny. I watched, not sure if I should root for my sister's success, since it would surely end in punishment or someone getting hurt. But Poppy became obsessed. She was going to get those shears no matter what!

After a while, the royal carpenter was summoned and instructed to build a special lockbox for the shears. When Nanny and the geese went to bed, Poppy tried to smash the box open. She stomped on it, even threw it out the tower window, but those shears stayed locked up tight. "One day," she declared. "One day I will have my own pair!"

The next week, we got to accompany our mother on an outing to the village. This was good news for both of us, because we loved exploring.

"If you are very well behaved," Mother told me, "we will stop at the Yarns and Noble store for some new books." Then she turned to Poppy. "And if you are very well behaved, we shall…" She paused. "Well, what would you like for your reward?"

"Shears," Poppy said.

"Sweetheart, you know you're not old enough for shears. How about a thronecake? Or fairyberry gelato? Or some fudge?"

Poppy glowered.

The first thing we did in the village was to drop the royal lion cubs at the groomer. Poppy and I had never been there, and Poppy gasped when we walked inside. There were shears everywhere! Big ones for trimming lion manes, tiny ones for clipping hedgehog nails. At one station, a white Pom-Pomeranian was getting its fur dyed pink. At another station, a long-haired wiener dog was getting a perm. Poppy started asking all sorts of questions, her eyes wide as saucers. "Mother, I don't want to go get fudge. Can I stay here and watch? Please, please, please?"

It was agreed that Poppy would stay at the groomer's, under Nanny Nona's supervision. I waved goodbye to Poppy, but she'd already grabbed a smock and was starting to help wash one of our lion cubs. She looked so happy.

Mother and I finished our errands, then bought some new books. When we returned to the groomer's, the cubs had big bows on their heads and Poppy was beaming. Over a plate of fudge, she told us all about it. "They let me shampoo and condition, and they let me paint nails."

"She didn't touch any shears," Nanny Nona reported. "I made sure of that." She patted Poppy's head. "She was a real help in there. I was very impressed."

The next morning, at the crack of dawn, Poppy shook me awake. "Look," she said. She opened her hands to show me a small pair of grooming shears.

"Where'd you get those?" I asked. "You didn't take them, did you?"

"The groomer gave them to me." She grinned. "Come on, let's go have some fun."

I knew we'd get into trouble, but I followed anyway. I didn't want to tattle on my sister. Besides, if she hurt herself with those shears, she'd need my help, so I had to take the risk.

The goats didn't know what to do when Poppy and I entered the barn. They'd never considered getting a beard trim, but Poppy told them that they'd look very stylish. She was very convincing. So they let her trim their beards into goatees. The results were lopsided. Those poor goats. The horses were next. When she was done, it looked as if she'd taken a beanstalk whacker to their manes. After working her way through the animals in the barn, she went outside and found the grandfather lion sitting beneath a tree. He was toothless, and agreeable, so she gave him a trim. It looked terrible, but lucky for her, there were no mirrors out there. The old lion strutted around, thinking he looked like the cat's meow.

I grimaced at the sight. Poppy had the enthusiasm, but spending one afternoon at the groomer's hadn't been enough training. Snip snip, snap snap, went the shears. It was lucky for us that it was super early and our parents weren't yet awake. But if anyone wanted to find us, all they'd have to do is to follow the trail of fur. "Let's go back," I pleaded. "If you get caught with those shears, you'll get into big trouble."

"Okay," Poppy agreed. But once we'd snuck back to our room she said, "Now I'm going to cut my own hair." She stood on the stool in front of our mirror.

This, I knew, was going too far. "Don't," I warned. "It'll look..." I didn't want to hurt her feelings but she was terrible at cutting hair. The worst! "It'll look... different."

"That's exactly what I want. Besides, I don't like long hair. It gets in the way of everything. And I don't need it. I'm not the next Rapunzel." Before I could stop her, she started cutting. I gasped as big chunks of hair fell to the floor. It looked like a dragon had taken bites out of her hair. And then she did something that almost made my heart stop. She cut her own bangs! Everyone knows it's risky to cut your own bangs. Though they were way too short, she smiled at her reflection.

When Nanny Nona came in a moment later, she took one look at Poppy and fainted.

It was not a pleasant morning in the O'Hair household. Poppy's haircut was bad enough, but when our parents realized that Poppy had been in danger, carrying a sharp cutting implement, things took a turn for the worse. Father was beside himself. He issued a royal proclamation that all shears were to be removed from the castle and from the village, then destroyed. "Nevermore will a pair of shears come near my daughter," he declared.

As it turned out, by reading all those fairytales, I'd picked up some wisdom. "Father," I said, "Sleeping Beauty's parents ordered all spinning wheels destroyed. But that didn't work."

"What are you saying?" he asked.

Mother put her arms around me and gave me a proud squeeze. "What your firstborn daughter is wisely saying is that you can't stop fairytale magic. Maybe Poppy has found her destiny." Then she pulled Poppy into a hug.

The very next day, Mother called Sir Stuart's School of Beauty and asked the question that would change Poppy's life. "Do you have any classes for children?"

# Zero Stars

When Holly finished her story, Apple clapped. "You're a fairy, fairy good storyteller."

"Yep, she's definitely a cut above the rest," Poppy said with a grin.

The cloud had dried most of Apple's hair. It hovered over her head, giving it a final puff of air. "Isn't it nice that being born without a destiny doesn't seem to be an issue anymore?" Apple said to Poppy. "You're figuring it out on your own. You're going to be a stylist to the spellebrities!"

"Well, I'm a stylist to Sparrow and the Merry Men," Poppy said with a chuckle. "It's a good start. Although, giving the Merry Men a new look isn't going to be easy. They are so stuck in the whole leather-studs thing."

"What about Sparrow's music?" Holly asked. "Can you help him with that?"

"His music does take some getting used to," Poppy agreed. "But his new songs are actually not that terrible." She was more adventurous with her musical tastes than Holly.

"As long as it's not like his last concert," Apple said. "All the glass goblets exploded. My ears were ringing for a week."

Holly watched her sister's reflection in the mirror. Had Poppy blushed a bit when mentioning Sparrow? Yes, she definitely had. Surely if Poppy had a crush on someone, Holly would know. Wouldn't she? They told each other everything. But the more Holly thought about it, she realized that Poppy and Sparrow had been spending time together lately.

As if reading Holly's mind, Apple asked, "So? Is there anything going on between you and Sparrow?"

"No," Poppy insisted, a bit louder than necessary. "We're just friends. It's fun hanging out in his tree house, listening to music. That's all."

Holly was relieved to hear this. Because she couldn't shake the feeling that Sparrow had been flirting with her in the stairwell. Even though she was most definitely not interested in him, it might hurt her sister's feelings if it turned out Sparrow liked her. She was resolute that no boy would ever come between them. Never ever after!

The cloud evaporated. Apple ran her fingers over her hair. "It's hexcellent," she said happily. "Thanks fairy much." She took off her little smock and tossed it into the laundry bin. A pair of blue songbirds flew in through the window and tucked two flowers into Apple's hair. When they'd finished, she grabbed her MirrorPad. "Oh dear," she said, glancing at the screen.

"What's the matter?" Holly asked.

"You have a new comment on your blog. And it's not fairy nice." Frowning, she handed the Mirror-Pad to Holly. Apple had been reading another one of Holly's stories. Titled "The Mouse Princess," it was a twist on the tale of the Swan Queen, the girl who is cursed by a sorcerer to be a swan by day and a human by night. To make it feel like a brand-new story, Holly had chosen to turn the queen into a mouse. And instead of setting it in a castle, she'd set her story in the middle of a bustling city. It was one of her most popular stories, as evidenced by the record number of positive comments.

But this one, added moments ago, was not positive. In fact, it was downright seething.

> Holly O'Hair might think it's funny to
> be turned into a rodent, but I'm not
> laughing. Some of us have serious
> destinies to deal with. We all can't be
> guaranteed perfect Happily Ever Afters!
> Maybe if Holly had to deal with a curse,

as some of us do, she'd think twice before writing stories like this. I give this story zero stars!

"Duchess Swan," Holly whispered. As the daughter of the Swan Queen, Duchess was taking the story *very* personally. "Wow, she's really mad. She thinks I was being mean."

"That's so unfairest," Apple said. "We all know you're not being mean. You're just being creative." Poppy nodded in agreement and placed a comforting hand on her sister's shoulder.

Holly didn't have a mean bone in her body. She'd wanted to create an entertaining story. But it hadn't occurred to her that someone's feelings might get hurt. She slumped in the styling chair.

"You're always going to have critics," Poppy pointed out, trying to make Holly feel better. "Everyone in creative fields has to deal with something like this sooner or later."

"Yes, I guess you're right," Holly said.

Apple set her MirrorPad into her book bag. "Well, Duchess is right about one thing. We *were* guaranteed Happily Ever Afters. Holly and I have our hexciting destinies, and Poppy gets to create her own. Fairytale magic is certainly wise and powerful." She blew two kisses. "Charm you later." And off she went.

Class must have finished over at the Red Shoes Dance Club because the music had stopped. The only sound at that moment was Clipper, snoring. Holly sat, very still, staring into the mirror. Poppy stood, equally still, behind her. Both sisters looked as if they'd been hit with a freezing spell.

*Fairytale magic is certainly wise and powerful.*

Holly had heard those words before. So had Poppy. Their gazes met in the mirror.

"Don't say it," Poppy said. "We've been over it a hundred times. We're not doing anything wrong."

"But we're messing with that magic." Holly's voice was a whisper. "We're messing with destiny."

Poppy's stubborn side took over, and she shook her head as if to clear her thoughts. "I don't want to talk about this again. We promised to leave it in the past. Nothing bad has happened. We've convinced everyone. There's no reason to reveal our secret now."

Holly knew her sister was right. They'd chosen their course. They'd made a vow to keep their secret. And everything was going perfectly right in their world.

But as a writer, Holly knew that no story was complete without some sort of conflict. As soon as everything looked perfect and rosy, something happened. Something always happened.

*Stop fretting,* she told herself. All was well. As Poppy swept up the strands of cut hair, Holly put her smock into the laundry bin. Then she gently woke Clipper. After hugging her sister, she headed out of the salon. But as she walked down the stairs, instead of humming, she repeated Poppy's words in her head.

*Nothing bad has happened. We've convinced everyone. There's no reason to reveal our secret now.*

She sure hoped Poppy was right.

## Growing Backward

When Holly awoke the following morning, the first thing she did was check her MirrorPhone. Alas, there were no missed calls from Edith Broomswood. No hexts or voice messages, either. Even though Holly knew Ms. Broomswood would need time to pitch the *Fairytale Fangirl* stories to publishers and publishers would need time to *read* the stories, she still felt a twinge of disappointment. This was surprising because Holly O'Hair was considered an expert on waiting. She'd gotten an A plus in all her waiting assignments in Princessology. Waiting was a big part of her storyline.

But this wasn't a prince she was waiting for. These were her stories. They'd come from her heart. She told herself to be patient. Good things come to those who wait.

She pushed the blankets aside, swung her legs out of bed, and slipped her feet into a pair of fuzzy slippers. Holly shared her dormitory room with Poppy. Their room was set in a tower that rose above the main student dormitory. There was concern, among her parents and the headmaster, that if Holly lived below, with the other students, she might forget what it was like to be in a tower, and that altitude adjustment could cause a shock to Holly's system when her tower imprisonment began. It was best that she stay acclimated to high places, where the air was thinner. Poppy had volunteered to be her sister's roommate, which had made Holly very happy. Not many people would choose to have to climb up all those stairs every evening after class, but Poppy did it without even thinking about it and never complained.

"Eeh! Eeh!"

Nor did her monkey complain. Along with a non-traditional wardrobe and hairstyle, Poppy also had a very unusual pet. Barber, a small squirrel monkey, scampered across the room and leaped onto the windowsill. "Eeh! Eeh!" he chirped. Poppy opened the window, setting him free to play in the forest.

Clipper stretched across the foot of the bed and yawned. Holly patted him, then grabbed her bathrobe, with its collar of faux lion fur. Because Clipper was charmed to stay a cub, he would never grow a full mane, which also meant that he'd never be king of the beasts. It was nice knowing that she didn't have to worry about him becoming the top of the food chain and eating other students' pets. Sometimes she wished she were also charmed to stay a teen forever. She'd never have to make tough decisions, like keeping secrets from those she loved.

A soft patter of rain fell on the windowsills. The

shower would last just long enough to green the gardens. Then the sun would peek out, as it always did at Ever After High. Because Poppy was still asleep, Holly tiptoed toward her closet. She knew exactly what dress she'd wear—the yellow one with the gold satin belt. But she paused midstride. Something felt different. What was it? Her head felt... lighter. She stopped dead in her tracks, in front of her vanity mirror. "Poppy!" she cried.

Poppy poked her head out from under a pillow. "What's the matter? Did I oversleep? Am I late?"

Holly spun around and pointed at her head. "It's shorter! Look!" Holly's hair, which had been cut yesterday to waist-length, now fell just past her shoulders. "What happened? Did you cut it while I was sleeping?"

Poppy rubbed her eyes. "Why would I do that?"

"Someone must have cut it." Frantic, Holly rushed to her bed and began to search the pillows for locks of hair. Surely there'd be evidence of this horrid crime! But she found nothing. "Clipper, did you see anyone?" Clipper yawned again. If there'd been an intruder, he would have protected Holly with his ferocious kitten growl. But there was no sign that anyone had entered the tower dorm room. Panic welled in Holly's chest. Her heart pounded. "I don't understand. How's this possible? If someone didn't cut my hair, then…" She gasped. "Hair can't grow backward! Can it?"

"Let me see." Poppy scrambled out of bed, but as she grabbed her purple bathrobe, Holly pointed at her.

"Oh my fairy godmother!" Holly cried. "Look at *your* hair."

"My hair?" Poppy's hands flew to her head. "What the hex?" Poppy rushed to her vanity. While Holly's hair had grown shorter, Poppy's had grown faster than usual. Way faster. It hung to her waist. And it was no longer purple. It was back to its natural auburn hue. Poppy and Holly stood side by side in utter shock, staring at their reflections. Nothing like this had ever happened. Their hair had always been as predictable as a sunrise.

"What are we going to do?" Holly asked, her hands flying to her head. This was not something that could be covered up like a pimple or erased like a misspelled word. This was major. "I've never had hair this short. I can't be seen like this!"

"There must be a hexplanation." Poppy grabbed her MirrorPad and began to search. "It says here that if hair stops growing or grows slower than usual, it could be caused by a vitamin deficiency. Did you stop taking your multivitamin?"

"No," Holly said.

"It says that it could be caused by stress. Have you been stressed?"

"Not really. I mean, I'm busy, but I'm always busy."

"What about this publishing thing? You sent your stories to the literary agent weeks ago. Did that stress you out?"

"Yes, a bit. But my hair isn't growing slower than normal. It's growing backward!" She tugged on her hair. "And what about you? What makes hair grow faster?"

"Let's look it up." Poppy's fingers flew across the screen. "It says that if you want to make hair grow faster, there are tonics you can take and magical spells you can cast. But I didn't do any of that stuff."

"Look up growing backward."

"Nothing," Poppy said.

Holly thought about it. "Try the word *ungrowing*." That sounded like something that would happen in Wonderland, which was a place where they celebrated unbirthdays and drank untea, which was simply water.

"I can't find anything. Let me try another magic word search." Poppy tried again. Then she looked at the screen and scowled. "It says here that hair growing backward could be a curse."

"Of course!" Holly stomped her foot. "Someone cursed me. That's what happened. But wait, who would do a thing like that? I don't have any enemies. Do I?"

"I don't think so." Poppy set her MirrorPad aside. "Okay, so maybe this is a class assignment, you

know, for General Villainy. They're always doing things like this. Remember when they had that Next Top Villain contest?"

"You're right," Holly said. "But I just can't believe those students would curse me. I always try my best to be kind, and I can't think of anything I've done to deserve this. I'm going to go downstairs right now to get to the bottom of this." The words "going downstairs" made Clipper jump to his paws.

"You want me to come?" Poppy asked.

"Can you stay here and watch Clipper? Last time he was down there, he tried to catch Lizzie Hearts's hedgehog and he got prickles in his nose."

"Okay," Poppy said, picking Clipper up and hugging him tight. "Good luck."

Holly's robe billowed behind her as she hurried down the stairs and onto the main floor of the girls' dormitory. She knew exactly who to ask.

Faybelle Thorn, daughter of the Dark Fairy and president of the Ever After High Villain Club, was one of the most outspoken villains on campus. If there were any villainous activity going on, she'd know. But Holly was well aware that one of the most dangerous things she could do would be to anger a dark fairy. So she couldn't outright accuse Faybelle of cursing her. She had to tread lightly with her questions. Faybelle was also the captain of the cheerhexing team, and if Holly upset her, Faybelle could make Holly's practice sessions miserable.

After taking a long breath, Holly knocked on Faybelle's door. It flew open. "What do you want?" Faybelle asked coldly.

Holly wasn't surprised to find that even though it was still very early in the morning, Faybelle was already dressed and ready for the day. The fairy had to be extra organized, since she had as many hextra-curricular activities as Holly. "Hi, Faybelle," Holly said sweetly.

Faybelle put her hands on her hips. "Well? I'm waiting?" Faybelle had a notoriously hot temper and was known to toss fairy dust whenever the mood

struck her. If some of that dust landed on Holly, she might grow an extra ear or a tail.

"Well, I was wondering…"

Faybelle's wings unfurled. Holly stepped back with alarm. Faybelle flew into the hall and zipped around Holly. "What's up with your hair?" she asked snippily.

"Would you believe I cut it?" Holly asked.

"Don't mess with me, Holly O'Hair." Faybelle zipped around again. "I've asked you countless times to cut your hair so the other cheerhexers wouldn't trip over it. But you've always said that growing your hair long was your destiny. You'd *never* cut it short. What's the real story?"

"Uh, yeah, well, that's why I came to see you."

Faybelle landed on the floor, then folded her wings. "I'm listening."

Holly swallowed nervously. Even though she'd spent a lot of time with Faybelle, she still felt uneasy around her. There was always a flicker of threat

behind Faybelle's eyes, and the knowledge that, at any moment, she could fire the fairy dust. "Do you have any new assignments in Villainy class? You know, to like, uh, curse other students?"

"I wish," Faybelle said. "I'd love to curse some of those Goody Two-shoes who are really getting under my wings."

"So, no curse?"

"No." Faybelle raised an eyebrow. "But I'm happy to consider an offer if you'd like one?"

"Thank you but no thank you," Holly said, quickly making her retreat. "See you later, at practice." She wished she had a pair of wings so she could get out of there faster. Faybelle's intense gaze practically seared a hole in Holly's back as she hurried down the hall. She rounded the corner and was about to head past another door.

---

DUCHESS SWAN
LIZZIE HEARTS

---

Holly stopped in her tracks as Duchess's bad review came back to mind. Maybe if Holly had to deal with a curse, like some of the others, she'd think twice before writing stories like that.

*Could Duchess Swan have cursed me?* she wondered. It was possible. Duchess had a big chip on her shoulder about those who were destined for Happily Ever Afters. But unlike Faybelle, who embraced her villainous roots and loved making others feel uncomfortable, Duchess wasn't a classic villain. Yes, she was one of the General Villainy students, but she didn't have evil parents or even a plan to conquer the world. And she wasn't a witch or a sorceress, so she'd have to go to great lengths to cast a dark magic spell. Holly couldn't ignore the possibility. She took a deep breath and knocked on the door.

"ENTER!" shouted a voice.

Holly opened the door and came face-to-face with Lizzie Hearts. As the daughter of the notoriously bossy Queen of Hearts, Lizzie was a big fan of shouting. In fact, one of her favorite sayings was

"When in doubt, shout!" The two girls knew each other, for they'd spent many days together in Princess-ology and Kingdom Management.

"Oh, hi, Holly." Lizzie was pinning her crown to her red-and-black locks. "What happened to your hair?"

Holly could feel herself blushing. "Um, well, I'm trying something different. It's temporary." Her gaze darted around the room. "Is Duchess here?"

"No. She's away at a dance recital." Lizzie opened a drawer and removed a teacup. Then she held it at arm's length. "TEA!" she hollered. A teapot flew out of her closet and filled her cup. "Would you like some?" she asked Holly.

"No thank you." Holly lifted her foot so that Lizzie's hedgehog could waddle past. "Lizzie, I was wondering, since you and Duchess are roommates, is there anything that I should know?"

Lizzie took a sip of tea. "Whatever after do you mean?"

"Is Duchess...mad at me?"

"Well, she really didn't appreciate your story about the mouse princess, if that's what you're getting at."

"Yes, I know. I read the comment. I wish she wouldn't take it personally. It's fiction."

Lizzie set her teacup aside. "Duchess takes *everything* personally. She gets her feathers ruffled all the time."

Holly fiddled with her bathrobe, nervous about asking this next question. "Do you think she's mad enough at me to do something about it?"

"You mean, like revenge?" Lizzie carefully applied a layer of deep red lipstick to her already red lips. "It's possible. Duchess is a perfectionist. She wants to get the best grades in school. I'm sure Mr. Badwolf would give her hextra credit if she pulled off a feat of revenge." Lizzie rubbed her lips together and made a smacking sound. Then she smiled at Holly. "But she's not here, so you don't have to worry. However, just in case, you might want to sleep with one eye open." She grabbed her flamingo scepter.

"Well, I'm off to Anger Magicment. Riddle you later!"

Holly hurried back up the stairs. "There's no cursing assignment in Villainy class," she reported when she'd returned to the tower room. She almost didn't recognize her sister. Without the short purple hair, it was as if Holly was looking at herself standing across the room!

"Well, I don't see how hair growing backward could be anything but a curse," Poppy said. "Have you done anything lately, anything at all that might have made someone mad at you?"

"Duchess Swan is mad at me. But she's away at a dance recital."

"What about making someone jealous. Or, I don't know, *anything?*"

Holly thought for a moment. She would never hurt anyone's feelings on purpose. And most everyone told her that being stuck in a tower sounded super boring, so she couldn't imagine that anyone was jealous of her or her destiny. "Nothing comes to mind. What about you?"

"Nothing."

Holly and Poppy both sat on the edge of their beds. Clipper brushed against Holly's legs, but Holly was so lost in troubled thoughts, she didn't pet him. "What if...?" she whispered, unable to say what she was thinking. But she didn't have to. Her sister knew.

"No," Poppy said, shaking her head. "Don't start in on that again. I don't believe it."

Holly kept her voice quiet. "But what if...what if our hair is trying to tell us something?"

Poppy laughed, but it sounded forced. "Hair doesn't talk. It doesn't communicate."

"Okay, so maybe that's true but—"

"*Maybe* that's true? I work with hair every day. If it could communicate, I'd know." Poppy didn't usually get annoyed with her sister, but her tone was a bit impatient. Holly knew right then that her sister was feeling equally scared and frustrated.

Holly stood and slowly began to pace. "Okay, so hair can't communicate, but what if the fairytale magic that rules our hair can? What if that magic is trying to tell us something?"

"And what's it trying to tell us?" Poppy asked.

Even though Holly knew they were alone, and even though she knew no one could hear their conversation from way up in the tower, she still looked around to make sure she hadn't missed an eavesdropper. Cleaning fairies were known to get caught in drawers and closets, but they usually made loud buzzing sounds when trapped. She checked the closet anyway, just to be sure. Then, feeling safe, she said the words that Poppy didn't want to hear. "Maybe the magic is trying to tell us that we should accept our birth order."

Poppy darted to her feet. "I absolutely refuse to believe that," she said. She stomped over to her vanity and grabbed her beloved shears. "I don't believe that fairytale magic, or fate, or whatever you want to call it, gets to choose. I'm stronger than fate, and I choose." Then Poppy began her morning routine of cutting her hair into its asymmetrical bob. As she grabbed a tube of purple hair dye, she stomped into the bathroom. Before the door closed, she said, "I've spent my whole life making my own decisions and I'm not going to change that now."

Holly sighed. She loved her sister's determination, her confidence, her absolute certainty that she could control her destiny.

But what if she couldn't?

Holly opened her bedside drawer and rummaged through the papers and receipts until she found a particular photo. As she stared at it, her thoughts drifted back to the day when the truth had been revealed and when everything she'd believed about herself had become a big fat question mark.

## Chapter 7

## Birth Order

Secrets are strange wild things that fight against their very existence. Try to contain them and they will strain the seams, weaken the ropes, wear down their jailer until they are released. Thus far, Holly and Poppy had kept their secret safe, locked up tight like a girl in a tower. No one knew. No one.

Except Nanny Nona.

It had happened last year, during the twins' legacy year at Ever After High. One morning, the twins had been going about their usual routine, getting ready for classes. Holly's class, Kingdom Management, began super early. Poppy didn't have to attend this class, since she wasn't destined to rule a kingdom.

"So yesterday, in Princessology, Apple recited the girls' royal headwear line from birth tiara to coronation crown from memory," Holly said.

"That's fableous," Poppy said as she tied her scarf.

Then the school bell rang. Holly grabbed her books. "Hey, little sis, see you after class at the Tower Hair Salon."

"Love ya, big sis," Poppy said after a hug goodbye. With a wave, Holly hurried out the tower door.

*Holly's heels clicked as she hurried down the long flight of stairs. All was well in the world. She was ready to study, to prepare for her future role as queen. But alas, the class turned out to be a boring lesson on taxation. And to make matters worse, she'd sat next to Briar Beauty. Holly liked Briar, but when Briar started yawning, Holly started yawning, and they'd both fallen asleep. Apple politely woke them so they wouldn't miss the thronework assignment. When class was over, Holly made her way to the Tower Hair Salon for her appointment.

While Poppy trimmed Holly's hair, she appeared distracted and didn't partake much in the conversation. Holly wondered what was going on. She began to tell her sister about a funny incident with Apple. "So then I told Apple, I know your story better than anyone ever after, and it was a Red Delicious apple that…" She paused. Poppy was clearly distracted. "Is something on your mind?"

Poppy bit her lower lip. "I…uh…hey, check out my new hair dryer." She quickly placed the dryer over Holly's head. It seemed that Poppy didn't want to talk about whatever was bothering her. Holly knew to give her space. If it was important, her sister would eventually share it.

But later that day, while Holly was taking Clipper for a walk, her MirrorPhone buzzed. It was a hext from Poppy.

## Meet me at Mad Hatter's, ASAP.

Holly sensed something was wrong. They'd had no plans for tea that day. Her schedule was jam-packed, but if her sister needed her, she'd be there without hesitation. She dropped Clipper at the Creature Day Care Center, then hurried to meet Poppy.

When Holly arrived at the Mad Hatter of Wonderland's Tea & Hat Shoppe, it was crowded with other students and villagers. Poppy was already seated, with a full tea service on the table—a purple teapot, mismatched cups and plates, and a cake stand with two thronecakes and two fairyberry scones. Poppy was always full of energy, but that afternoon she seemed downright fidgety. "Maybe you shouldn't drink any more tea," Holly advised. "All that caffeine does tend to give one jitters."

"It's not the tea," Poppy said after taking a sip. A yellow teapot flew out of the kitchen and landed on another customer's table. Holly had to duck out of its way. "There's something I need to tell you."

"Uh-oh," Holly said. The serious expression on Poppy's face was worrisome. "What in the ever after is the matter?"

"Maybe you should eat something." Poppy offered a scone. "I don't think you should hear this on an empty stomach."

Holly sat up straight. "Now I'm really worried. Is Clipper okay?" Poppy set the scone onto a plate and poured tea into Holly's cup. "Is someone sick? Is it Mom?" All sorts of bad thoughts came into Holly's head. "Is Dad sick? Is it you?" No, that wasn't possible. If Poppy were sick, Holly would instinctively know.

"Mom and Dad are fine, too. And so am I."

Holly sighed with relief. A pair of sugar cubes danced across the table, then jumped into her cup. A spoon flew over and stirred her tea. She decided to try to cheer up her sister. "I heard that in Hero Training class, Daring scaled a tower, just like in his story and…" She paused. Poppy was staring down at the table. "Okay, I'm totally getting a twin vibe that you are not telling me something. What is it?"

Poppy furrowed her brow. "Okay, you know when you know something but you can't—"

Suddenly, all the clocks in the Mad Hatter's shop went berserk, dinging, donging, and chiming. The noise was nearly deafening.

"Guess we can't talk now!" Poppy hollered, barely audible above the racket.

Before Holly could reply, her MirrorPhone buzzed in her pocket. It was her scheduling alarm. "Oh dear!" she shouted. "I'm going to be late for cheer-hexing practice!" Faybelle would get her wings into a tizzy if any members of her team were late. She leaned across the table so her sister could better hear her. "Poppy, can whatever this is wait a little bit? I mean, if you, Mom, and Dad are all okay, whatever it is can't be that time sensitive, can it? Can we talk later? Right after practice?"

"Sure, we can do that," Poppy said. "It's fine. It'll be fine." She gave her sister a tense smile and crammed a scone into her mouth.

Holly hugged her. "Don't worry. Whatever is

upsetting you, it will be okay. I promise." And off she hurried.

During cheerhexing practice, Holly was distracted, thinking about her sister. As soon as Faybelle dismissed the team, she hexted Poppy to tell her she was available again to talk. They met in the library.

"Okay, tell me now," Holly said as she tossed her pom-poms and book bag onto a chair.

Poppy set her hextbook aside. Her face was pale, her expression uncommonly serious.

"Are you in some sort of trouble?" Holly asked. "Did someone complain about a haircut? Did you get fired?" Even though that could never happen in a million years, because Poppy was the most amazing stylist the Tower Hair Salon had ever employed, Holly still had to ask. What else could have made her sister so upset?

Poppy opened her mouth, but a group of students entered. They began pushing tables and chairs closer together for a study session for Chemythstry. Poppy groaned. "I don't want to tell you, not with this many people around." Then her MirrorPhone chimed. "I have to go," she said. "I've got an appointment at the salon."

"But—?"

"You know, now that I've had time to think about it, never mind. It's really not important. I'll figure it out." She smiled bravely, then hurried away.

This was so frustrating! Holly grabbed her Mirror-Pad and linked to a MirrorCast show called *Just Right*, created and updated by Blondie Lockes, daughter of Goldilocks. Blondie was the school's reporter. If there were any news about Poppy, Blondie would know. She got the scoop on everything. Holly scrolled through the list of headlines. But Blondie's latest entries were about how Raven Queen, daughter of the Evil Queen, and Dexter Charming, second son of King Charming, had been spotted having dinner together at the Green Bean Garden in Book End. There were dozens of comments speculating on the nature of that get-together. Was it a date? Did they like each other? Did kindhearted Dexter have a chance with the daughter of the most evil villain who'd ever lived? Normally, Holly would have found this discussion very interesting, but she couldn't stop thinking about her sister.

Five o'clock came. She waited in their tower room, listening for Poppy's footsteps on the staircase. Finally, Poppy entered. Holly rushed to her side. "I'm still getting a twin vibe that something is fairy wrong. What is it?"

Poppy took a long, deep breath. Then she looked straight into her sister's eyes and said what she'd been hiding all day. "Nanny Nona called this morning, after you left for Kingdom Management."

"And?"

"And she told me something, something that could change our lives forever."

"I'm listening."

"She...well, I'm not sure how to tell you this, so I'm just going to say it. She mixed up our birth certificates when we were born."

Holly was certain she'd heard her sister wrong. "Mixed them up?" she repeated.

"Well, she got confused. There was so much going on. No one had expected twins, as you know, so when the first baby was born, that baby was wrapped in a pink blanket that had been made especially for the heir. The blanket had the O'Hair crest on it. When the second baby was born, that baby was wrapped in a plain pink blanket. The royal butler took a picture." Poppy grabbed her MirrorPad. "Nanny Nona sent me a copy." The MirrorPad's screen lit up, showing a photo of a somewhat perplexed-looking Nanny holding a pink-wrapped infant in each arm.

"We've seen that before," Holly said, trying to keep her voice even.

"Yeah, I know. But now take a look at this photo." Poppy swiped the screen and another picture appeared—the first official royal portrait. "The first-born is wearing a gold crown, the secondborn is wearing a silver crown." Holly nodded. She'd seen this photo every day of her life. A larger version hung in the castle's library.

"I don't understand," Holly said. "What do these photos have to do with our birth certificates?"

"Look," Poppy urged. She pointed to the butler's photo. Holly leaned closer. Poppy was pointing to the baby in the plain pink blanket. "Look at the right side of her head."

It wasn't easy to see, but a small wild hair curled above the infant's right ear. Holly gasped. "What? That's *my* hair. But that means…" She grabbed the MirrorPad and swiped back and forth between the first photo and the second photo. "I'm in the plain pink blanket. And then I'm wearing the golden crown."

"Exactly," Poppy said. "You were born *second*. You were named Poppy. I was born first. I was named Holly. But when Nanny gave us baths, she mixed us up, and she gave you the golden crown and she gave me the silver crown. And it's been that way ever since. So when she went to fill out the birth certificates, your footprint and your handprint were stamped onto the certificate for Holly O'Hair, first-born daughter of King and Queen O'Hair."

"I'm *Poppy?*" Holly felt a weight press upon her shoulders, as if the ceiling were trying to crush her. She slumped onto the desk chair. "Why didn't Nanny tell us? Why didn't she fix this?"

"She only just realized her mistake. Apparently she was putting together a scrapbook for Mom's birthday, and she found the first photo. She said it had been many years since she'd looked at it. And for the very first time, she noticed the wild hair."

Holly's eyes filled with tears. What sort of terrible turn of events was this? She started to cry. Poppy grabbed a tissue and handed it to her. "This means… this means…" She couldn't finish the sentence.

Poppy frowned and gave her sister's hand a gentle squeeze. "This means that I'm supposed to be the next Rapunzel," Poppy said sadly. "I know this is difficult for you to hear. I'm not one bit happy about this, either."

"But I *like* being the next Rapunzel," Holly said softly.

"And I like being…something else."

They sat quietly for a very long time. To find out that you aren't the person you believed yourself to be, that you'd spent your entire life preparing for a future that wouldn't come, well, that was a major blow. Holly was not a future queen. All those years of tower schooling, the braiding, the boring Kingdom Management classes—had it all been a big waste of time?

"What's going to happen to us?" Holly asked finally.

"That's what I've been trying to figure out," Poppy told her. "And I think I've come up with an answer." She grabbed another tissue and dabbed Holly's eyes. "Nothing is going to happen. Nothing is going to change."

"What?" Holly stared at her sister. Did Poppy not understand the gravity of their situation? "Poppy, how can you say—?"

"Shh, let me finish," Poppy said gently. "Only three of us know the truth—you, me, and Nanny Nona. She said she wouldn't tell anyone. That it was up to us to break the news. I think she's a little afraid that Father is going to be very angry. That she might get fired." While the king wasn't known for having a hot temper, this wasn't a small mistake. "The butler's photo is the only evidence."

"Are you saying we should destroy the photo?"

"Yes," Poppy said, nodding her head firmly for emphasis. "We'll tell Nanny Nona to destroy the original. And we will *never* tell anyone the truth. We'll keep things status quo. I don't want to be the heir, but you do. This way, we can both have the destiny we want."

"You mean, *deceive* everyone?"

Deception was a harsh-sounding word, but perhaps there was no sugarcoating it. "Yes, I guess that's what we'd be doing. But it's for the right reasons." The sisters looked into each other's eyes. They would do this.

Poppy grabbed her MirrorPhone and pressed Nanny Nona's number. Nanny's rosy-cheeked face appeared on the screen. "Nanny, are you alone? Can you talk?"

"Yes," Nanny said. She adjusted her spectacles. "Have you told your sister?"

Holly squeezed next to Poppy so that both of their faces appeared on the screen. "Hi, Nanny. Yes, Poppy told me."

"I'm so very sorry, my dears. I'm afraid I've made a big mess. Now everything will change. It's going to upset everyone. I've been preparing my letter of resignation." She sniffed and wiped a tear. "I should start packing my bags."

"No, Nanny, there's no need for drastic measures," Poppy said. "Holly and I think that everything should remain hexactly the same. Nothing should change. I don't want to be the heir, and Holly is very happy with her destiny. We want you to tear up the butler's photo. Throw it away, and pretend it got lost a long time ago."

"But what about fairytale magic?" Nanny asked. She rubbed her hands in a worried way. "You might be able to fool the world, but you can't fool fairytale magic. It chose you, Poppy, to be firstborn for a reason."

"We've gone this long, and fairytale magic hasn't seemed to care," Poppy pointed out. "So we vote

92

that we leave things as they are." Holly nodded in agreement.

Nanny Nona started to say something and then stopped herself. "I know how stubborn you two can be. My, my, well, if that's your decision. I'll be so happy if I don't have to resign. I don't know where to find a job at my age."

And so it was that the twins and their nanny made a pact. It was the first time they'd kept something from their parents, from their friends. From the world.

At the time, Poppy had felt confident that it was the right thing to do, but Holly hadn't been so sure. However, she trusted her sister and didn't voice her doubts. She accepted their new reality and tried hard not to worry about it.

But now, one year later, Holly's doubts were back, and they were stronger than ever. Not worrying was no longer an option.

# The Royal

## Student Council

*O*nce a week, the Royal Student Council gathered in the Great Hall. The five council members—presidents, vice president, secretary, and treasurer—met at a table beneath an oak tree that was so massive, its branches had pushed through the hall's arched ceiling. If the tree could talk, and sometimes it did, it would recount tales of the generations of royals who'd sat beneath its boughs, discussing important matters of the day. The tree remembered when chivalry had been all the rage and when the topic of debate had been whether or not the expectations of chivalric behavior should be extended to non-royal students. The tree remembered last century's blizzard, when the entire school had disappeared beneath the snowdrifts and giants had to be summoned to dig everyone out. And there were the discussions that cropped up, generation after generation, like whether students should wear school uniforms, whether they could have unsupervised parties, and when would somebody do something about the Castleteria food?

Holly was the first to arrive. Because of the whole "hair growing backward" incident, she'd missed her Princessology class, but she wasn't going to miss Royal Student Council. While Poppy had managed to look normal again, by cutting and dyeing her hair, Holly was stuck with shoulder-length locks. It was so embarrassing. The *only* thing she was expected to do was to grow amazing long hair. That was it. If anyone found out that her hair wasn't growing, she'd be mortified. So she'd come up with a convincing story. And hopefully, everyone would believe it and her hair would be back to normal tomorrow.

Poppy wasn't going to make the meeting. She was going to spend the lunch hour doing some research, to see if she could find out anything about backward-growing hair. She'd hext Holly if she found an answer.

Holly made her way to the table, stepping over a few tree roots. She'd left Clipper at the Creature Day Care Center, so she didn't need to worry about him climbing up into the tree and then getting stuck, like last time. After settling into the fourth chair, she checked her MirrorPhone for the ump-teenth time. No messages or missed calls from Edith Broomswood. And nothing from Poppy. She set the phone to buzz, then placed it on the table so she could keep an eye on it. She then arranged her other items—the official student council ledger and a small well of ink and quill. Her main role, as secretary, was to take notes during the meeting. It would have been much easier taking notes on a

MirrorPad, but because the Royal Student Council was steeped in tradition, Headmaster Grimm insisted that traditional recording methods be used. He was a stickler for doing things by the book. Thus, the notebook was leather bound, the black ink came from ground dragon scales, and the quill was a griffin's feather.

Humphrey Dumpty, son of the famously unbalanced Humpty Dumpty, was the next to enter the Great Hall. Being of a nonathletic nature, he had a bit of trouble negotiating the tree roots, but after only one tumble, he sat in the chair next to Holly. "Hi," he said.

"Hi. Uh, your crown's a bit tilted," she told him politely.

"Oh, thanks." He adjusted his crown. Some might call him a nerd or a brainiac. The tree might say that the old term was *egghead*, but truthfully, Humphrey was one of the smartest Crownculus students at Ever After High. That's why he'd been elected Royal

Student Council treasurer. As treasurer, Humphrey kept track of all monies collected and spent by the council. "What did you do to your hair?" Humphrey asked after staring at Holly for a long moment.

"Poppy cut it," Holly said. This was her first chance to try out the story. "She's working on her portfolio, so she needed a model."

"It looks nice," Humphrey said. He seemed to have accepted the story because he didn't ask any more questions. He set a leather-bound ledger onto the table, along with an inkwell and quill. His quill brushed against his nose, and he sneezed. "Excuse me." He sneezed again.

"Bless you," Apple called as she hurried into the hall. This year, Apple and Madeline Hatter shared the president position, but Maddie couldn't attend this particular meeting because she was helping her father inventory his teapot collection. As student council co-president, Apple took her role very seriously. She'd had a special sash made. She also had a lot of swag that she liked to give out, like cardboard cup holders, MirrorPhone covers, and apple-shaped stickers, all with the words *Stay Fairest*.

"Hi, Holly. Hi, Humphrey," she said as she spread the swag on the table.

"Hi," they both replied.

"Oh wow." She looked at Holly. "I've never seen your hair that short."

"Poppy needed a model, so I let her practice on me. For her portfolio. I was happy to offer." Holly nervously tapped the quill, waiting for Apple's reaction.

"Well, it's not traditional, but it looks good on you. And if you don't like it, it's no big deal because your hair will grow back in a few days, right?"

"That's true," Holly said, faking a smile of utter confidence. "My hair *always* grows back."

As Apple took the third chair, students began to arrive. Council meetings usually attracted a small, dedicated audience. They settled themselves onto benches that faced the table. Blondie Lockes sat on the front bench, MirrorPad in hand. She rarely missed a meeting. If anything interesting happened, it would make the headlines on her blog and on her MirrorCast show. She looked curiously at Holly. "Why the new hairdo?"

"Poppy wanted a model for her portfolio, so I offered. It will grow back in a few days."

Blondie's gaze fell upon Holly's phone. She raised an eyebrow. Was it obvious that Holly was waiting for an important call? Holly slid her phone into her pocket. She didn't want Blondie spilling the news about the literary agent—not yet. And she certainly didn't want her seeing a hext from Poppy about backward-growing hair.

"*Sparrow's in the HOUSE!*" Sparrow sang as he entered the Great Hall. He hit a couple of eardrum-shattering chords. A branch split in two. A window shattered. A bird roosting in the oak tree was so startled, one of its droppings landed on Humphrey's suspenders.

"Ew," Humphrey said, wiping it away with a hand-kerchief.

"SPARROW IN THE HOUSE!" Sparrow sang. Then he plopped onto a bench. "Hey, Holly!" he called. "Your hair is CRAY-ZAY!"

Holly politely waved. Then she tapped her quill again, waiting for the meeting to begin so everyone would stop talking about her hair. If only she could sit behind the tree trunk and take notes, then no one could stare at her. She ran her hand down her hair. Hold on, had her hair gotten even shorter? Her heart skipped a beat as she tried to casually tug on the ends of her hair to gauge whether or not it was actually shorter than it had been the last time she'd checked. What if this *was* a curse? Some kind of terrible dark magic? Duchess Swan wasn't on campus, but that didn't rule her out entirely. There was still a possibility that she was behind this. Perhaps she paid an evil witch to cast a curse remotely.

Headmaster Grimm drew everyone's attention as he strode into the hall. Dressed in his usual dapper attire, with a waistcoat and cravat, he cast a watchful eye over the audience. "Good afternoon, students," he said in his baritone voice.

"Good afternoon, Headmaster," the students responded. A special leather chair awaited him, somewhat resembling a throne. He took his seat, folded one leg over the other, then pointed to his pocket watch.

"It's time to begin," Apple announced. One empty chair remained at the council table. "I guess we'll have to start without the vice president." Holly dipped her quill into the ink, then began to write. "Hear ye, hear ye, hear ye," Apple called. "The Royal Student Council will come to order. Commence with roll call. Secretary O'Hair?"

"Here," Holly said.

"Treasurer Dumpty?"

"Here," Humphrey said.

"Co-president White?" Apple cleared her throat. "Here!" she said. "Please note that Co-president Hatter and Vice President Charming are absent."

"Have no fear, for I am here!" a voice announced.

A squeal arose from some of the girls in the audience. They were members of the Daring Charming Fan Club, and the object of their infatuation had entered the hall and was currently striding toward them. He had just come from a jousting class, so he was wearing a puffy white shirt and tight black pants. He leaped over the tree roots as gracefully as a show horse, his perfectly coiffed blond hair bouncing as if in slow motion. He stopped briefly to check his reflection in a mirror, then sat next to Apple. "Sorry I'm late," he said. "I had a wardrobe malfunction."

Apple leaned close to him, squinting. "Where? Your outfit looks fine to me."

"*That* was the problem. I look so *fine* in everything, I couldn't decide what to wear." Then he delivered his signature smile, which had recently been banned from all magic carpet–ports, due to its tendency to momentarily blind onlookers—pilots included.

As Daring's perfectly white teeth lit up the room, Holly quickly closed her eyes. She'd known Daring her entire life, so she'd had plenty of experience with his smile. Their parents were dear friends, and they'd been on many family outings together.

"Now that the vice president has arrived, let's get back to business," Apple said. She cleared her throat again. Then she paused with a puzzled look. "Holly, would you read back the minutes for our meeting thus far?"

Holly set her quill aside, stood, and began to read her notes. "Once upon a time, in a school for the sons and daughters of fairytale characters, a group of civic-minded students gathered to discuss matters of importance and to ensure that the voices of their fellow students were heard. As the clock struck midday, Co-president Apple White, looking as lovely as ever after in a red satin dress with a gold-foil filigree print, paired with pearl-white heels with bow details, thumped her gavel upon the oak table and declared that the meeting should come to order. Those assembled took heed, eager to hear the council's business. Roll call was issued, with Secretary Holly O'Hair and Treasurer Humphrey Dumpty in attendance. Holly's shorter-than-normal haircut was *not* due to any type of malfunction, but was a simple matter of helping her sister practice cutting a shoulder-length bob." Holly paused to stress this point. "Humphrey wore a bright green pair of suspenders and matching bow tie. Vice President Daring Charming arrived late, insisting that he'd had a wardrobe malfunction. He looked perfect, as usual."

"Why, thank you," Daring said.

"You're welcome." Holly turned the page in her ledger. "That's as far as we've gotten." She sat down and held her quill at the ready.

"Thank you." Apple pounded the gavel again. "Now we move on to the agenda." She picked up a piece of paper. "We've got a lot to cover in an hour."

One by one, they waded through the agenda items. Royal Student Council was a safe place where students could issue complaints about this and that. At this particular meeting, Gus Crumb, who was lumpy-porridge intolerant, wanted Hagatha, the school's cook, to offer a choice of lump-free porridge. Apple agreed to discuss the matter with Hagatha.

Holly found it difficult to concentrate. She desperately wanted to check her phone, but Blondie's keen eyes didn't miss a thing. Blondie was constantly on the hunt for news, like a hungry griffin searching for its next meal. If Edith Broomswood didn't call soon, would that mean the publishers weren't interested? She shivered. It was a dreadful feeling when doubt crept in, like falling into a cold, murky swamp.

"The next item is our fund-raiser for the Creature Day Care Center. Most of us have pets that we leave at the center, and it's in need of new flooring, new scratching posts and nests, and a paint job. Last week, we decided to hold a concert to raise money. Sparrow Hood offered to perform the music with his band, the Merry Men. Sparrow, do you have a report for us?"

"*SPARROW HOOD and the MERRY MEN!*" Sparrow sang. Everyone winced. A tree branch rustled, and another white blob landed on Humphrey.

"Not again," Humphrey sighed.

Sparrow leaped out of his chair and shot to the front of the hall. "Hey, Council," he said to the council. "I'm totally ready. Got some new tunes that'll ROCK YOUR CROWNS OFF!" He looked at Daring. "Or your tights."

"They are not called tights," Daring said, extending his leg. "They are called male hosiery, and I wear them for jousting."

"Whatever after. As I was saying, new tunes. And Poppy's gonna give us a new look!" He played a few chords, then slid across the floor until he landed in front of Holly. "Hope to see you there, O'Hair." And then he winked at her. Luckily, his back had been turned to Blondie, so she hadn't noticed the wink.

Okay, there was no longer any doubt in Holly's mind that Sparrow was flirting with her. It was so obvious. She hadn't done anything to encourage this behavior. And with everything else that was going on, this was really bad timing. She diverted her attention to the ledger, ignoring his gaze.

After a few more agenda items, which included a petition from the Track and Shield Team to ban the Croquet Team from the athletic field, due to the fact that the croquet balls, aka hedgehogs, were digging holes and causing the runners to trip, the meeting adjourned. Apple and Daring walked out together. Humphrey hurried away, intent on changing into new clothes. Sparrow, Blondie, and the others began leaving the Great Hall. Holly checked her phone. No hexts. She was about to call Poppy, to see if she'd discovered anything, when a loud voice startled her.

"Ms. O'Hair, I wish to speak with you." Headmaster Grimm stood before her, his hands folded behind his back, looking not one bit pleased.

# Some Nimble Advice

It wasn't unusual for the headmaster to wear a stern expression. His job was to maintain order, so he constantly supervised the students and their activities. He was also charged with overseeing the day-to-day details of the school. It was a workload that would make anyone cranky.

"Ms. O'Hair," he repeated.

Holly rose from her chair. "Yes, Headmaster?"

Due to his impressive height, Headmaster Grimm had the tendency to look down the bridge of his nose when talking to students. "I wanted to commend you on taking your duties as student council secretary seriously."

"Thank you."

"However…" He unclasped his hands and raised an index finger in the air. "While I appreciate your writing abilities, it is not necessary to be so *creative* when you take notes."

"Oh?" She sighed. Was that why she hadn't heard from her new literary agent? Did the publishers think she was too *creative*?

"Rather than embellishing, just stick to the facts," he advised. "That will save time *and* parchment."

"Okay, I understand." She nodded, but she didn't really understand. Why not make boring notes more interesting? If anyone had to go back and read the minutes from the student council, why not tell a riveting tale?

"One other thing, Ms. O'Hair." He stroked his mustache. "It has come to my attention that you've been writing a blog called…" He paused.

"*Fairytale Fangirl*," she reminded him.

"Precisely. I recently fielded a complaint about a particular story."

"Someone officially complained?" Holly winced. "I'm sorry about that, but a writer can't please everyone," she said. "There are always critics."

"This particular student was not a mere reader being critical, Ms. O'Hair. The story was about her family, and it deeply offended her."

Holly gulped. Duchess Swan, of course.

"In order to investigate, I visited your blog and read a few of the stories: the one about Snow White and the skiing dwarves, and the one about the mouse princess. Snow White does not ski in her story, Ms. O'Hair. And the princess turns into a graceful swan, not a furry rodent." He made a tsk-tsk sound. "Why do you feel the need to change what has already been written?"

"Why?" The answer seemed obvious to Holly. "To make them more entertaining, of course. I'm not changing the destinies, Headmaster Grimm, or the heart of the stories. Just the circumstances. I'm just using a little creative license." She smiled hopefully at the headmaster, but his expression remained stern.

"The point I am making is that, while fairytales do change from generation to generation, there is no need for *you* to change them. Each fairytale character must be responsible for making his or her own changes." He smoothed his waistcoat. Then he gave her a long look, the kind a parent gives after catching their child being naughty. "I suggest that you terminate your blog."

"Terminate?" It felt like one of Hagatha's lumps had caught in her throat. "But I love my blog."

"Then stick to your own story, Ms. O'Hair. That is a better use of your talent." And off he strode.

"Hold on," she wanted to call out. "You're asking me to stifle my creativity!" But she didn't. To question the headmaster was to question the school itself—at least, that's what she'd been taught. But she didn't agree with him, so what should she do? As she pondered this conundrum, she corked the inkwell and set it, along with the quill and ledger, into her book bag.

"I respectfully disagree with our headmaster," a voice said. Startled, Holly nearly dropped her bag. Someone was still in the Great Hall? She narrowed her eyes and peered toward the back of the room. She spotted a chair that was somewhat hidden by the tree's shadows. A pair of bone-thin legs stretched beyond the chair.

"Professor Nimble?" she called. "Is that you?"

"Indubitably." The professor had a distinct voice, an octave higher than most, and all his sentences rose on the last word, as if they were questions. Holly picked up her bag and made her way past the benches until she was standing in front of the professor. She'd gotten to know him this year because he taught Tall Tales, her creative writing class.

"Why do you disagree?" she asked.

"You are not stepping out of bounds by creatively reimagining other fairytales. Your duty, as a writer, is to be true to your nature. As an avid fan of fairy-tales, it makes perfect sense that they would become your genre." He stood, straightening his long limbs. His clothes hung loosely, for there was very little meat on his bones. He'd wrapped a belt twice around his waist to hold up his pants but still, they looked like they could fall off at any moment. He was the skinniest man Holly had ever known. "And by changing the circumstances, or details, of a story, you make it more exciting. What fisherman ever told the truth about the size of his catch? What knight didn't exaggerate the strength of the dragon? Without embellishment, no one would want to read."

Holly completely agreed with her professor. But, as a dedicated Royal, she very much wanted the headmaster's approval. "Headmaster Grimm thinks I should change my writing, or terminate my blog."

"Asking a writer to change her voice is like asking a fairy to stop flying." He set a black top hat onto his head, then patted it in place. "It is not a choice, whether to write or not to write. You are compelled, as are all true writers. This is your passion, Ms. O'Hair, and you must do your best to ignore those who wish to stifle you." He bowed. "See you in class."

As she watched her professor nimbly step over tree roots as he exited the Great Hall, she clutched her book bag to her chest. She agreed that writing was her calling. But how do you ignore a critic who might have cursed you?

After eating a quick lunch in the Castle-teria—a golden-egg-salad sandwich and a fairyberry smoothie—and after stopping by the Creature Day Care Center to hug Clipper, Holly hurried to her favorite class. Along the way, she stopped in the washroom to wash her hands. As she stood at the sink, with its golden spouting unicorn faucet, she looked in the mirror. For fairy's sake, it was true! Her hair had lost another inch since that morning.

Her MirrorPhone rang. She nearly tore her pocket as she yanked the phone out. "Hello?"

It was Poppy. "I don't have any answers about our hair, but I do have some amazing news. Sparrow's aunt is the fashion editor for *Fairytale Fashion Week* magazine. He told her all about me and how I'm going to be the stylist for his band. She said that a band makeover is the perfect subject for her magazine. She wants to do a photo shoot!"

"Wow!" Holly momentarily forgot about all their troubles. "I'm totally flipping my crown, Poppy! Congratulations! That's the best news ever after!"

"You see?" Poppy said. "This is another sign that we were right to keep our secret. I'm meant to be a stylist, not the next..." She paused, then lowered her voice. "Not the next Rapunzel. And you're meant to be the princess, trapped in a tower, writing and writing while you wait for your Happily Ever After. Speaking of writing, did you hear yet?"

"No."

"Don't worry. You will. They'd be stupid not to publish you. And don't worry about our hair dilemma. We'll figure this out."

Holly put away the MirrorPhone. She took one last glance at her shortened hair. Her sister always knew how to calm her down. They would figure this out. They were a team.

The Tall Tales classroom was located on the main building's topmost floor, requiring stairs, of course. C.A. Cupid, daughter of the Greek god Eros, flew past. She glanced over her shoulder. "Oh, hi, Holly, I didn't recognize you with that new hairstyle."

Cedar Wood, daughter of Pinocchio, was also making her way up the stairs. "I like your new look," Cedar said. As the daughter of the world's worst liar, Cedar was incapable of telling a lie, so Holly knew she meant it.

"It's just temporary," Holly explained. "It'll grow back to normal."

"I bet it's a lot easier to walk without all that weight on your head," Cedar said.

"It is," Holly said. Now she totally understood why her sister chose shorter hair.

The Tall Tales classroom was round, with windows offering a 360-degree view of the athletic field, the rooftops in Book End, and the mountains beyond. Holly tried not to stand too close to the windows. No matter how much time she spent in towers, she still got woozy if she looked down.

She sat at her usual desk, with Cedar on one side and Blondie on the other. Along with Cupid, the class included Bunny Blanc, Dexter Charming, and Kitty Cheshire.

Professor Nimble perched on his stool like a stick bug. Even though the room was heated by sunlight, the professor always seemed cold, hence his fingerless gloves and scarf. He clung to a hot cup of tea. "Good afternoon, writers." Holly loved that he called them writers instead of students. "Today we are going to discuss a powerful element in story—fate."

Some murmurs arose. MirrorPads were readied for note-taking.

"Who would like to define fate?" Professor Nimble asked. Cedar raised her hand. "Ms. Wood?"

"Fate is when something is destined to happen no matter what."

"No matter what?" As he blew on his cup of tea, his glasses steamed. His eyes disappeared from view for a moment, then returned. "Can you explain?"

"Well…" Cedar paused before responding. "Fate is very powerful, and if it decides that you're going to spend your life as a wooden puppet, then that's the final decision."

"You speak as if fate were a living, thinking entity," the professor noted.

Cupid raised her hand. "Where I come from, many people believe that fate is alive."

"That's crazy," Kitty Cheshire said.

"It's an important part of mythology," Cupid said. "You see, there are three Fates, and they control the thread of life, from birth to death. Three days after a child is born, the Fates visit the house and determine how long that child will live. One of them spins the thread of life on her spindle. The other measures how much thread each person gets using a measuring rod. And the third Fate cuts the life thread with her shears." She adjusted her pink headband when she was done speaking.

"Write this down," Professor Nimble said. "Fate, or destiny as it's also known, is a supernatural power that chooses a course of inevitable events that will lead to a predetermined outcome. That outcome can be good or bad." He looked around the room. "Some of you hold tightly to the belief that your life is dictated by fate, while others don't. That very debate has been heard in these hallowed halls for centuries. But no matter which side of the fence you stand on in real life, as writers you get to decide whether or not fate plays a role in your story."

"But doesn't it play a role in everyone's story?" Dexter Charming asked.

"That is the question you must ask yourself." Professor Nimble set his teacup aside.

Holly raised her hand. "Professor? My parents

always talk about fairytale magic and how it decides things. Is that the same as fate?"

"Yes, it's the same concept, just another way to describe it." Professor Nimble began to pace in front of the class, his long arms folded behind his back. "If you believe that fate is unalterable, that it is a piece of thread waiting to be snipped at a specified time, then you might write a story about a hero who tries to outwit fate. The result would be tragedy, for no matter what she does, she cannot change her destiny."

Holly took very precise notes. *No matter what she does, she cannot change her destiny.* She reread those words. She furrowed her brow. By pretending to be firstborn, she was clearly trying to outwit fate.

"However," Professor Nimble continued, "if you believe that fate or fairytale magic is merely a concept and it has no actual power, then you will write a story about a hero who makes her own decisions and the tragedies or the victories that ensue are the result of free will." He stopped pacing and turned briskly on his feet. "Questions you might ask

yourself: Is falling in love chance or fate? Is being born first chance or fate?" Holly looked up from her note taking. She swallowed hard. Then she raised her hand again. "Yes, Ms. O'Hair?"

"Is it?" she asked. "I mean, is being born first chance or fate?"

"That is not for me to answer. You are the writers— you decide."

*Yes, but I'm not talking about a piece of fiction*, Holly thought, *I'm asking about real life.*

Holly's hand fiddled with the ends of her hair. "Professor Nimble, if the writer believes in fairytale magic, but the hero tries to trick it, does it take revenge?"

"That is a very interesting question, Holly. But the answer is for you to decide. Your assignment, class, is to write an essay about the role of fate."

It was an interesting assignment and usually Holly would be thrilled. Tall Tales thronework was always her favorite because it never felt like work—not like Kingdom Management thronework, where she had to memorize the difference between micro and macro-economics, or Princessology thronework where she had to practice waving to her royal subjects. But Holly wasn't certain she wanted to write this particular essay. It brought up a lot of scary questions.

Class was dismissed. Everyone scuttled down the stairs. Holly's MirrorPhone rang as she was heading out of the building. "Holly, dearie?" Edith Broomswood's shrill voice was unmistakable. "I have news." Then her face appeared, too close as usual, making the wart on the tip of her nose look like a mountain. Holly's heart began to pound. What kind of news? Her legs turned to jelly, and she leaned against the wall, steadying herself for what might come her way. "An editor at the renowned publishing house Simon and Pieman read and, I quote, adored. He said your writing is filled with youthful zeal. She said it's so refreshing that you aren't telling the same old stories! She wants to publish you. Holly, are you there? Are you listening?"

Holly could barely speak. The words wouldn't come. She nodded wildly at the screen.

"She wants to meet you. She wants us to come to her office in Camelot. What are you doing tomorrow?"

Excitement began in the tips of Holly's feet and flew right up her spine. She squealed so loudly, it echoed down the hall. Blondie appeared immediately, MirrorPad ready to record. "Is someone squealing about something?" Blondie asked, looking around.

Holly took a deep breath, then spoke the words she'd longed to say. "I'm getting published!"

That evening, the twins shared the news with their mother. Well, not *all* the news—just the good stuff.

"I'm going to be the stylist for Sparrow Hood's upcoming concert and his aunt is a fashion editor for *Fairytale Fashions* and she's coming out to do a photo shoot. If she likes the results, she'll publish it in her magazine," Poppy said.

"And an editor from Simon and Pieman wants to meet me tomorrow and talk about publishing my stories into a book," Holly said.

Queen Rapunzel's smile was so warm, the screen actually steamed up. "Oh my darlings, I'm so proud of both of you. What wonderful news. I can't wait to tell your father."

"Mother?" Holly took the phone from Poppy's hand and looked into Rapunzel's green eyes. "Headmaster Grimm doesn't like my stories."

"Really?" Rapunzel's brow furrowed. "Did he say that?"

"He wants me to either stick to my own story or stop my blog. Actually, he used the word "*terminate*." I'm not sure what to do."

"What do you mean you're not sure what to do?" Poppy asked. Holly hadn't yet shared this news with her. "He can't tell you how to write your stories. They belong to you."

"But he's the headmaster. I don't want to be disobedient." Holly waited for her mother's wisdom, but Rapunzel's reply surprised her.

"I agree with Poppy," Rapunzel said. "While the headmaster has jurisdiction over the goings-on at

127

Ever After High, he does not have authority over your creativity. He is a good man, and I appreciate his steadfast resolve to uphold tradition, but I do not like censorship. Your father and I wholeheartedly support your talents—the talents of both of you."

Holly nodded. She knew her parents would support her, but it was disheartening to think that her art would run counter to the headmaster's wishes.

Poppy put an arm around Holly's shoulder. "If you're going to be a published writer, you're going to have to get a thicker skin. You can't let critics change you."

"Yeah, I guess you're right." Criticism didn't seem to affect Poppy the way it did Holly. Poppy had spent most of her life doing that which wasn't expected—surprising, opposing, and simply being contrary. None of those verbs were usually associated with Holly.

Rapunzel folded her arms and stared into the screen. "So?" she asked with a raise of her eyebrows.

"Is one of you going to tell me what's going on with your hair?"

Holly's hand shot to her head. She looked at her sister. Poppy stepped in. "I'm just trying some new stuff," Poppy said. "Holly was nice enough to let me practice on her."

For a moment, Holly held her breath. The twins were already keeping one truth from their mother, and now they were telling another lie.

"Well, you know that I support your artistic endeavors, Poppy, but can't you find other models? Holly's hair is a symbol of our family. She is expected to have the longest hair on campus."

"Yes," Poppy agreed. "I get it. I'll practice on someone else."

Rapunzel and Holly discussed the arrangements that needed to be made so that she could leave campus to visit Simon and Pieman. Rapunzel sent a permission slip to the headmaster's office. "Now I must run off to a meeting of the Historical Guild.

They want to raise the ticket price to my tower, to help fund repairs. We had a record number of tourists last year, and it's starting to show wear and tear. Bye-bye, my darlings." Rapunzel blew two kisses, and the screen went black.

Holly set her phone aside, then collapsed onto her bed. So much had happened that day, and she was exhausted. Tomorrow she was going to meet a real-life editor from a real-life publishing company.

Poppy filled a bowl with monkey kibble. Barber bounded across the bed, grabbed the bowl, then retreated to the highest shelf, where he could eat without having to worry about a playful lion cub. "Don't you have thronework?" Poppy asked Holly.

"Yes," she replied. If only tomorrow could appear in the blink of an eye. Clipper licked her face. She hugged him, then dragged herself to her desk. With all her excited thoughts, how would she focus on the work at hand? Her dream was about to come true!

But her gaze traveled from her desk and out her window, at the darkening sky. As a storyteller she knew that all stories needed conflict. If the hero's dreams seemed to be coming true, something bad was bound to happen. Otherwise, the story would be boring. And often, the writer left hints that the bad thing was coming—little shadows here and there that foretold of the darkness that was on its way.

Holly looked at her own shadow on the wall. She reached up and touched her hair.

Was it trying to tell her something?

## *Hairy* Magic

"AHHHH!"

That was the first thing Holly said the next morning. It wasn't actually a word, but in its volume and length, it conveyed the message that something was terribly wrong!

She stood in front of her vanity, her face whitened by shock. Her hair. Where had it gone? It hung just one inch past her jaw. And it was purple!

"AHHHHHHHH!"

"What's happening?" Poppy cried, bolting upright in bed. Her gaze darted around as if she expected to find a dragon climbing in through the window. She'd clearly been in a deep sleep because she looked as disoriented as an upside-down pixie. She rubbed her eyes. "What's going on?" Barber pushed his nightcap away from his eyes and squeaked.

"AHHHHHHHHHHH!" It was all Holly could say. Words had abandoned her. Her calm demeanor shattered as she stood, flabbergasted by the sight of her reflection.

Poppy threw back her covers and tried to scramble out of bed, but instead, she got tangled in something and tumbled to the floor. "What the hex?" she grumbled. Holly spun around and gasped at her sister. As Poppy had tumbled, so too had a mass of auburn hair. It spread around Poppy like a cloak. "I can't see anything!" Poppy struggled to get all the hair out of her face. When she'd finally pushed it away, she tried to stand, but it was wrapped around her legs.

Holly opened her mouth to scream again, but stunned silence fell over her. The astonishment was almost too much to bear. She sank onto her vanity bench.

"What's the deal with all this hair!" Poppy complained as she struggled to get to her feet. Finally, success! Then she looked down at her feet. The thick auburn locks hung all the way to the floor, not a streak of purple to be seen. "Oh. My. Fairy. Godmother!"

Holly began breathing quickly. Her heart pounded. This had to be a dream. She pinched herself. Clipper watched from the end of the bed, his head cocked in puzzlement. She pinched herself again. "This can't be happening," she whispered.

"Stop pinching yourself," Poppy said. "This is real." She gathered her hair and flung it all over one shoulder. Then she stumbled across the room. "It's so heavy, I can barely walk."

Holly's voice rose with frustration and fear. "Why aren't you devastated? Why aren't you screaming? Why are you acting as if nothing has happened?"

"It's not going to do us any good if we *both* freak out," Poppy calmly told her. She sat on the other vanity bench. "I'm just as puzzled as you."

"Look how short it is," Holly said, tugging at a lock. "What if it keeps getting shorter and I end up *bald*?"

"No O'Hair has ever been bald." This was true, not even the men. Not even Great-Grandpa O'Hair, who'd lived to be one hundred and seventeen years, and though his red locks had turned silver, they were still as thick as a horse's mane on the day he took his last breath.

"Maybe no one's gone bald...*until now*!" Holly said. "My hair is growing backward!"

She burst into tears, and nothing Poppy said consoled her. Clipper's purring didn't make her feel better, either. Finally, when her eyes were all puffy and her nose red, she grabbed a box of tissues. "Okay, I'll stop crying now. I know it's not helping. But we have to do something. I'm supposed to leave for Camelot in..." She glanced at the wall clock. "In one hour!" She started pacing. "What if my hair grows backward during our meeting?"

"Okay, let's think this through." Poppy chewed on her lower lip as she thought. Her eyes narrowed. "I don't think this is anything physical, like stress or a virus, because it's affecting us totally differently."

"Yes, that makes sense."

Poppy tapped her fingers on the edge of the bench. "The only explanation is that this is magic. I mean, look, your hair turned purple without hair dye. But what kind of magic, that's the question? Bad magic or good magic?"

"It's bad magic, obviously," Holly said. "I'm going to be bald, probably by tomorrow!"

"It's not the Villainy students, you checked that out. And the only person you can think of who is upset with you is Duchess Swan. I'm beginning to think she's behind this!"

"But Duchess isn't a spellcaster."

"She could have gotten some help from a sorcerer."

"But casting dark magic against another student is against the rules. If she got caught she'd get hexpelled. Duchess wouldn't risk that. She's way too serious about her grades." Duchess was a straight-A student, and ranking top in her class was extremely important to her.

Poppy nodded. "That's all true, but this is *Duchess* we're talking about. You know how mean she can be. And you know how she feels about princesses with Happy Ever Afters. It's very possible that she's our culprit." Poppy grabbed her MirrorPad and scrolled through her calendar. "Duchess has a hair appointment with me tomorrow. You'd never believe the kind of things people confess when they're getting their hair done. If she's behind this mess, I bet I can get her to admit it!"

Holly grabbed another tissue and blew her nose again. "But what if it's not Duchess? What if *someone* isn't cursing us? What if it's *something?*"

Poppy frowned. "I already know what you're going to say, and I totally disagree."

Holly hurried to her desk and grabbed her notebook. "There is a tradition in storytelling—if the hero tries to fight her destiny, it brings about her downfall. In this case, we're the heroes and we're fighting our destinies by pretending to be who we're not."

Poppy tightly folded her arms. "Firstly, I'm not pretending to be who I'm not. I'm being the *real* me. And secondly, that is storytelling, not real life."

"Our life *is* a story," Holly said.

"So you think that fate or destiny or fairytale magic, or whatever you want to call it, is mad at us and cursing us?"

"Yes! The magic that rules our story is making my hair grow short because I'm not supposed to be the next Rapunzel."

"Okay, so if you're correct, then that would mean that fate is more powerful than free will? Do you really believe that?"

"Have you looked in the mirror?" Holly knew her sarcasm wasn't helping. She tried to calm down by taking a long, deep breath. "I'm not sure what I believe. Until Nanny Nona told us about the birth certificate mix-up, I believed with all my heart that I was destined for one thing. But now…"

Poppy stood up. "Magic isn't going to tell me what I can and cannot do!" She grabbed her favorite shears. As Holly watched, wide-eyed, Poppy cut a section of hair from her head. But as the hair fell toward the floor, it vanished in midair and the cut section immediately regrew. "What?" Poppy cut another section. The same thing happened. "Ugh! This is so frustrating." She cut again, at lightning speed, but each time, the old hair vanished as it fell to the floor and a new lock grew in its place. No matter how much she cut, she still had long hair.

But Poppy would not be defeated. "Okay, so what?" she said with a stomp of her foot. "So my hair is long and your hair is short. That doesn't change anything. Even if we can't find a way to end this curse, you can still be Rapunzel's heir, and I can still be whatever I want to be."

"Don't you see?" Holly said sadly. "There are some things that can't be changed. This isn't my *Fairytale Fangirl* blog. This is real life. And in real life, Jack *always* climbs the beanstalk. Cinderella *always* loses her glass slipper. And Rapunzel *always* grows long hair."

The sisters looked into each other's eyes. Silence filled the room. Even Clipper and Barber sat still, as if they knew that something bad had happened.

A knock on their tower room door broke the silence.

"Holly? Dearie? It's Edith Broomswood!"

## Chapter 13

# An Unexpected Visitor

dith Broomswood, literary agent extraordinaire, stood outside Holly's dormitory door.

"What's she doing here so early?" Holly whispered. Her heart began to pound again. "We're not supposed to leave for another hour. She can't see me like this."

Ms. Broomswood knocked again. "Holly? Let me in." She sounded breathless. "Those stairs were murder on my joints. And it's as cold as a troll's nose out here."

Holly knew it would be terribly rude to keep her brand-new agent waiting in the cold. And with all those spiders who lurked between the stones in the tower's stairwell. "I'll pretend I'm sick," she whispered. "I'll tell her I can't go to the meeting."

"You can't do that. This is too important to reschedule." Poppy pushed more hair from her eyes. "I'll pretend to be you. I'll say hi, and then tell her that I need to get dressed and I'll meet her downstairs."

"What? But you haven't pretended to be me since we were kids."

"I can do it," Poppy said, but there was no twinkle in her eye. This wasn't like tricking the royal butler or the geese nursemaids. They both knew that a lot was at stake. Holly hugged her. They both put on the other's bathrobe, and then Holly watched as Poppy opened the door.

"Holly!" Edith Broomswood burst into the room, a human tornado of energy. She was short enough to be in Snow White's story. Her black hair, ratted and

piled on top of her head, somewhat resembled the hat she used to wear during her witch career. Her orange dress clung to her round body, making her look a bit like a pumpkin in heels. She took Poppy's hands. "My dear, you are the flea's knees. The crow's elbows. You look so much like your mother, though I've never met her, but I've seen pictures, of course." Then she scurried over to the window. "A dorm room in a tower. How fitting. And this is your sister?"

Holly held out her hand. "Hello," she said. "I'm Poppy." She was overwhelmed with excitement to meet this woman, but she tried to hide it by biting her lower lip.

"Love the purple hair." Ms. Broomswood scampered back to Poppy. "Now, before we meet the editor, there's one little question I need to ask."

"What's that?" Poppy said.

"I need to make certain that you are the real deal." Ms. Broomswood, who only stood as high as Poppy's waist, squinted up at her. "You *are* the real deal, right?"

"What do you mean, exactly?" Poppy asked.

"Do you promise that you are the author of your stories? That you didn't copy them from someone else. That no one can come forward once you're published and accuse you of plagiarism."

Poppy didn't need to look at her sister for the answer. "Of course Holly wrote those stories. I mean, of course I wrote them. Every single word."

"Hexcellent." Ms. Broomswood patted her fairy-hive hairdo, which was leaning a bit to the left. "Believe me, dearie, you don't want to get caught up in a nasty legal battle. Do you remember when Rumpelstiltskin wrote his memoir, *Short and Angry*? Turned out he'd lied about everything. He'd never been an orphan. He had a privileged childhood. His parents had raised him in a lovely castle in the suburbs and had sent him to private school. They sued for slander. What a mess!" Ms. Broomswood checked her Mirror-Phone. "Now it's time for you to get dressed. I want you looking the part of the princess. You must look like the next Rapunzel."

Holly, who'd been too nervous to speak, stepped forward. "Why must I...I mean, why must Holly look like the next Rapunzel?"

Ms. Broomswood turned to Holly and cackled. "Because it will help sell books! Rapunzel is one of the most famous fairytale princesses ever after. Simon and Pieman is very excited that her daughter has written the stories." She turned back to Poppy. "This is a once-in-a-lifetime opportunity. Do your best to look the part. I'll wait for you downstairs." And out the door she waddled. Holly peered out the tower window. A stretch royal carriage waited in front of the dormitory. A wave of dizziness hit her, so she turned away.

"Oh double hex," she said, sinking onto her bed. "Ms. Broomswood wants me to look the part. How can I with short hair?"

"Even if we had hair extensions that were long enough, which we don't, there's not enough time to attach them," Poppy said.

"Extensions wouldn't help anyway. My hair is *purple*," Holly reminded her. Clipper wound around her feet. She reached down and patted him. "The editor is expecting the next Rapunzel. I can't show up looking like this." Her eyes filled with tears again. "A once-in-a-lifetime opportunity only comes once in a lifetime. This is a total disaster."

"Fine. I'll do it," Poppy said. "I'll go to the meeting dressed like you."

"What? Wait? You will?"

"Of course I will. We can't let this stupid curse, or whatever it is, ruin your chances at publication."

Holly jumped to her feet and hugged her sister. "Thank you! Do you think I could come with you, to help in case the editor asks questions about my writing process?"

Poppy thought about this for a moment. "I think Mom would be fine with me missing school. I suppose I could reschedule my appointments, but—" And that's when Poppy's MirrorPhone rang. "Hello?" Poppy said. She listened, her eyes widening. "What? Right now? But I can't do it right now. I'm busy and..." She paused, still listening. "Yeah, okay." As Poppy hung up, her usually chipper expression turned sour. "You're not going to believe this."

"I'll believe anything right now." Holly braced herself.

"Sparrow's aunt wants to talk to Sparrow and me about the photo shoot. She's going to conference call Sparrow's tree house in thirty minutes. I'm supposed to get over there."

"But you're going to Camelot. I mean, I'm going to Camelot. This is so confusing."

"You'll have to go to Sparrow's for me," Poppy said.

"But I don't know anything about being a stylist for a rock band."

"And I don't know anything about being a writer of fairytales. But the only other choice we have is to tell everyone about our hair. And if people see that your hair is growing short and mine is growing long, they might put two and two together, and our secret will be discovered. And there's no way I'm going to start taking Kingdom Management classes and live with all this hair for the rest of my life. It's so heavy, it's going to give me a migraine!" Then Poppy forced a smile. She took her sister's hand. "We did this as kids; we can do it now. We'll get through this day."

"But what happens tomorrow if our hair is still mixed up?" Holly asked.

"We'll just keep pretending that everything is normal so no one gets suspicious," Poppy said with steadfast resolve. "We must see if we can reverse this on our own and continue to claim the paths we've chosen." She reached into her closet and grabbed a black knitted sweater tunic and some purple leggings. "Here, this is what you're wearing today."

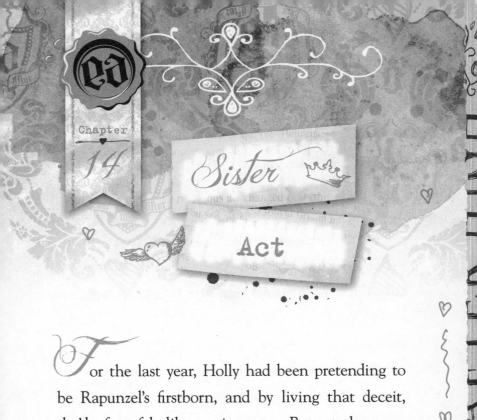

# *Sister* Act

For the last year, Holly had been pretending to be Rapunzel's firstborn, and by living that deceit, she'd often felt like an imposter. But, at the same time, she'd still felt like herself, her *true* self. Now, however, she'd become an imposter, 100 percent! Not only was she wearing her sister's hairstyle, she was dressed in purple leggings, a sweater tunic, and knee-high fringed boots. Poppy had added the final details—a colorful silk scarf and gold bangle earrings. As Holly stepped out of the dorm, a breeze

tickled the back of her neck. That was certainly a new sensation.

Poppy squeezed Holly's arm. "Good luck," she said.

"Same to you." Holly glanced over at Edith Broomswood, who waved from the limousine window. "Be sure to take notes," Holly told Poppy, handing her a notebook and quill. "Lots of notes. Don't forget to write down all the details, like everything the editor says, the way he says it, what the office looks like, all the stuff you see in Camelot...." Holly was going to go on and on, but Poppy smiled sweetly.

"How about I *tell* you instead of writing it down?"

"Okay." Holly couldn't be disappointed. Her sister was making an amazing sacrifice. She watched Poppy climb into the stretch royal carriage. It was like watching a movie of herself. Poppy's hair cascaded to her ankles. She wore Holly's favorite ruffled chiffon high-low skirt with a braided belt. Her headband was detailed with magnolia flowers. *This would make a great story for my blog,* Holly thought. *It might even be a funny story, if it wasn't happening to me!*

Poppy closed the back door, but being unused to having such long locks, she slammed it on her hair. She opened the door and, with a groan, pulled all her hair inside. A few moments after the carriage had started down the long driveway, it stopped and the back door flew open again. Poppy rushed out. "I almost forgot—we need to switch MirrorPhones." Of course! They switched, hugged, and then Poppy went through the whole slamming-hair-in-door routine again, and finally, she was off.

Holly put the quill and notebook into her book bag. She might have stood there for a while, feeling sorry for herself that she was going to miss out on meeting the editor and worrying that things might go awry. Sure, she had confidence in her sister, but what if the editor started asking all sorts of writing questions? That could be tricky for Poppy. But a chime alerted her to a hext from Sparrow.

Where are you? it sang.

On my way, she hexted back.

Like the other Ever After High students, Sparrow Hood had a dormitory room on campus, but he mostly hung out in his special tree house, on the outskirts of campus. Sometimes he even crashed there. Holly guessed that the headmaster had approved this living arrangement because it fit with Sparrow's destiny to be an outsider, living in the woods, just as it fit with her destiny to sleep in a tower. Most everyone was happy that Sparrow spent a lot of time out there. If he'd been in the dorm, his late-night practice sessions would have kept most of the students awake.

The forest critters, however, didn't seem happy to have Sparrow as a neighbor. Close to campus, the trees were thick with birdlife, and the thicket was a happy home to squirrels and rabbits. But all signs of these critters disappeared the closer Holly got to the tree house. She couldn't blame them. The guitar riffs made the ground shudder and branches shake. Surely there were trees that could be planted to magically absorb the noise pollution. Or perhaps

someone could make tiny bird-sized earplugs and pass them out. She made a mental note to bring that up at the next Royal Student Council meeting.

Despite the unpleasant *music* emanating from within, the tree house was a lovely work of art. Perched at the top of two massive fir trees, deep in the forest canopy, it was built from an assortment of scavenged materials—an old barn door, abandoned castle windows, even the hull from a ship. To reach the front door, one had to ascend a wooden staircase that wound around and around one of the trunks.

"Hey, Poppy," Sparrow called down to her, sticking his head out the door. "Hurry up. It's time to ROCK AND ROLL!"

Holly picked up her pace. She ducked beneath a branch, then stepped inside. The interior wasn't as delightful, and was badly in need of a professional decorator. A faded rug covered some of the patch-work floor. The furniture consisted of beanbag chairs, an old stained couch, and a bunch of mismatched pillows. A stage had been set up in the back half of the room, with all the Merry Men's equipment. Soda cans and chips bags littered almost every surface.

One of the Merry Men was draped across the couch, reading some sheet music. The other two were making sandwiches in the corner kitchen. They were dressed like Sparrow, with green leather pants and studded black boots. All the Merry Men were students at Ever After High, but she'd never been formally introduced to them, so she didn't know their names. But she was very familiar with Sparrow's story, so she did know the Merry Men's legacies. They were the children of Friar Tuck, Little John, and Will Scarlett.

"Hi. I'm Hol…I mean hi, I'm Poppy," she said to them. They each gave her a puzzled look.

Sparrow scratched his soul patch. "They know who you are. Did you fall on your head or something?"

"Hey, Poppy. I'm guessing you want your usual." One of the Merry Men standing in the kitchen tossed her a can of fairyberry soda. Holly caught it.

"Thanks," she said. The usual? How often did her sister hang out here?

"Hey, I'm working on a new song." Sparrow grabbed his guitar. "It was inspired by a *certain girl* at school." He began to sing. "*HOLLY! You're my FOLLY. Let down your HAIR! I don't mean to STARE! But you've caught me…*" He stopped.

Oh pickled peppers! This was total proof that he liked her. There was no doubt about it now.

"*But you've caught me…*" he sang again.

"Unaware?" she offered.

"Oh, that's good. *UNAWARE!*" He plucked more chords.

Holly opened the can of soda. She was parched after that long walk. "So, you're writing a song about my sister?"

He grinned. "Yeah. I never paid much attention to her, but after talking to her on the stairs, I'm totally inspired. There's something about her. *HOLLY! I'm just a GUY! You make me SIGH!*"

Holly cringed. As far as poetics, Sparrow probably wouldn't be the next William Shakespell. In a way, she was flattered. No one had ever written a song for her. And now that she looked at him close up, he was sort of cute, in an unkempt and wild way. But eventually, she'd need to tell him that she wasn't interested. Seriously, there was way too much going on in her life to start dating someone.

A flash of light drew her attention. The wall mirror lit up, and a young woman's face appeared. "Sparrow?"

"Aunt Heather!" he said. He set the guitar on its stand. "Poppy just got here. Poppy, this is Heather Hood, my father's sister."

"Nice to meet you, Poppy." Aunt Heather looked a bit like Sparrow, with the same shaggy brown hair and green hues in her clothing. A diamond stud sparkled on her right nostril. "I'm hexcited to hear your ideas about Sparrow's new look. Give me a moment while I take this last shot." She turned away from the screen. She was in a studio. Her three models were cats that were standing on their hind legs and wearing boots. Aunt Heather put a camera to her eye. "Okay, I want hissy fit. Give me hissy fit!" The cats began to hiss. Their tails twitched.

The shutter on Heather's camera clicked. "That's it. That's purrfect."

Holly took the opportunity to whisper to Sparrow. "Did Poppy—I mean, did I tell you any of my ideas for the new look?"

"No," Sparrow said. "You said it was going to be a surprise. Are you feeling okay? You're acting different. How come you didn't kick off your boots like you always do?"

"My feet are cold," she lied. "You sure I didn't give you any hints? Like how I might do your hair? Or the kind of outfits I'm planning for you?" Sparrow shook his head. How was she going to bluff her way through this? This was Poppy's big opportunity!

"Okay, take a break," Heather Hood told her models. The cats sauntered offscreen. Heather set her camera aside, then perched on a stool. "Poppy, I've heard so much about you. Did you know that I started cutting hair at a little salon, just like you? But then I got a break styling a commercial for Wee Willie Winkie's Waterpark, and now I'm working for *Fairytale Fashion Week*. But I know what it's like being the secondborn. My brother got all the glory, and I had to make a name for myself. I admire your drive."

"Thank you," Holly said.

"But before I haul my crew and all our equipment out to your school, I'd like to know what we'll be shooting. Tell me about the new look you're going to create for Sparrow and the Merry Men."

Holly wanted to disappear. If only she could cast an invisibility spell. Amid the chaos of the last couple of days, she and Poppy hadn't discussed Poppy's vision. Sparrow looked at her. The Merry Men looked at her. Aunt Heather looked at her. The cats hissed in the background. What could she say? She couldn't blow this for her sister.

She thought about it in literary terms. Books were categorized by genre, and their covers had a certain look depending on the genre. For instance, a romantic fairytale cover looked different from a terrifying horror story. So, too, it was with rock bands.

Members of a princely boy band dressed differently from members of a troll grunge band.

"Sparrow, how would you describe your music?" she asked.

"Poppy, what is up with you? You're one of our biggest fans, aren't you?"

Holly realized her mistake and quickly tried another approach. "Of course I *know* how to describe your music—I mean, I listen to it all the time. But how would *you* describe it?"

"Oh, in my own words? Let's see..." He grabbed his guitar again. "I'd say it's sorta classic rock and roll, with a punk edge, and an alternative vibe, mixed with soul, sweat, and TEARS!"

That wasn't quite what Holly was hoping to hear. He clearly had no idea what his sound was. "Okay, try this," she suggested. "When people hear your music, what do you want them to say? How do you want them to react?"

"It would be nice if they didn't plug their ears," one of the Merry Men said with a snort.

"Yeah." Sparrow nodded. "That would be a nice change."

Holly sighed. She had nothing. No ideas. She tried to stall. "So, what I understand is that Sparrow's music doesn't fit into any categories because it's… *unique*."

"Yeah, that's it," Sparrow said. "That's what I want people to say about our band. Those guys are UNIQUE!"

"Then his new look will be…unique." Holly smiled sheepishly.

Aunt Heather nodded. "Unique is good. But unique how? What, exactly, will they be wearing? This is *Fairytale Fashion Week* magazine, not some student publication. I'm not going to shoot a feature if the work isn't worthy."

Holly shuffled in place. "It will be different. You know, distinctive, uncommon…" Yeesh, how many synonyms could she come up with for "unique"? "One of a kind." Aunt Heather frowned. She clearly wanted details. Holly was suddenly reminded of the fairytale The Emperor's New Clothes. When tasked to create a new look for the emperor, the tailor came up with nothing, but he pretended that he had made the most amazing clothes ever. He told the emperor that only those with exceptional sophistication could see the clothes. So while the emperor was actually parading around in a pair of long johns, everyone told him he looked marvelous. If Holly were writing her blog, she'd twist that tale to this very situation. Instead of a tailor, it would be a stylist, and instead of an emperor, it would be a wannabe rock band. A jolt of inspiration shot down Holly's writing arm. Her fingers twitched. She was dying to run back to her dorm and write the story. She'd take something very simple and make them think it was…the bee's knees!

"Classic," she said. "Classic Hood."

Aunt Heather stroked her chin. "Go on."

"No one will expect it. We'll evoke the days of the Sherwood Forest, the classic looks the Merry Men wore. Rustic colors, hats with feathers, tights—"

"Tights?" Sparrow exclaimed.

Aunt Heather narrowed her eyes. "It's risky."

"The new look will be very *retro*," Holly said, still stalling.

"Retro," Aunt Heather repeated. "That could work." The cats began meowing in the background. Then one of them made a strange hacking noise. "Great, a fur ball," Heather said with a roll of her eyes. "I'd better get back to my models. Put some sketches together and send them to me as soon as possible. I'm skeptical about this, but I'm still willing to give you a chance, Poppy. See ya later, Sparrow." The mirror went dark.

"Wait!" Holly cried. But Heather Hood was gone.

"What's going on?" Sparrow asked. "You know we don't want to look like our parents. We want something cool."

"Look, I'm having a really bad day. You've no idea," Holly told him. Had she ruined her sister's chances? Heather Hood had seemed unconvinced. "I'll make it work. Trust me." She was lying through her teeth and asking to be trusted at the same time. What a mess.

"Okay, I trust you." Sparrow grabbed a pair of drumsticks and beat them on the edge of the couch. He smiled at Holly. It was a nice smile. And he did seem like a true friend to Poppy. Despite the fact that he was destined to steal from royalty, she was beginning to understand why her sister liked hanging out with him.

Poppy's phone chimed. It was Poppy's calendar app, reminding her that she had an appointment at the Tower Hair Salon in ten minutes. For Duchess Swan! Yikes, was that today? How was Holly going to deal with this? This whole farce wasn't going very well, but she couldn't stop now. "I gotta go." Out of habit, she reached down to push her hair out of the way, but found only air. She hurried out the door. Sparrow followed.

"Hey, I was wondering, does your sister think I'm nice?"

"Yes, she thinks you're nice," Holly said as she headed down the stairs.

When she reached the last step, Sparrow called from the treetops, "Hey, do you think she'd go out to dinner with me if I asked?"

"Sure," Holly called. Why not? Poppy was very social. She went out to dinner with friends all the time.

But she didn't realize her mistake until she'd reached the edge of the forest.

Sparrow hadn't been asking about Poppy. He'd been asking about her! She'd just encouraged Sparrow to ask her out on a date!

## Swan

## Style

*D*uchess Swan had already arrived at the Tower Hair Salon. She was dressed for her afternoon dance class, in a sleek pair of dancer's pants and a stretchy top. She sat on the reception room sofa, perusing *Fairytale Fashion Week*. Her dance bag was tucked beside her delicate feet. "You're three minutes late," she grumbled. While Duchess wasn't a villain in the classic sense, she could certainly be uppity and ill-tempered.

"Sorry," Holly said, trying to catch her breath. The run from Sparrow's tree house had taken longer than she'd expected. As she inhaled, then exhaled, trying to calm her racing heart, she wondered, *How am I going to handle this?*

Holly had never cut anyone's hair. She'd always been the one being tended to, first by Nanny Nona, then the goose nursemaids, then the royal stylist, and finally by Poppy. Unlike her sister, Holly had never wanted to cut hair. Her natural inclination was to let it grow.

"Well?" Duchess said, tapping her foot. "Are you ready?"

"Am I ready?"

Duchess scowled. "Are you asking *me* if you're ready?"

"Yes. I mean, no. I mean, yes, I'm ready." Her thoughts reeled. What should she do? But Duchess had already grabbed a smock and was heading into the styling room. "Get seated and I'll be right there," Holly called. She clutched her MirrorPhone and dialed Poppy's number. Busy signal. She tried again, but the line was still busy. "Wait, what am I doing?" she whispered, realizing that Poppy's number was busy because she was using Poppy's phone. Royal fairy-fail! She dialed her own number, but it went immediately to MirrorMail. Poppy was probably in the middle of the meeting with the editor. Beads of sweat appeared on Holly's forehead. She needed styling advice, and she needed it now.

There were two other stylists in the salon, but they were busy with clients in another room. They waved at her. She waved back. She sat at the reception desk and began to look through the drawers. "Sweetie, whatever after are you doing?" It was one of the other stylists, a man named Barry. He'd walked out to the reception area.

"I'm looking for records. For Duchess Swan. So I know how she likes her hair."

He snorted. "When did *you* ever keep records?" Barry asked, tapping his leg with a comb. "You hate writing things down." He pursed his lips. "You look totally stressed. Clearly you haven't had your morning hocus latte. Be a love and order one, and then order my usual while you're at it." With a turn on his heels, he went back to his client.

Order his usual? She groaned. She dialed Hocus Latte Café. "Hi, this is Holly…" Ugh. She had to stop doing that! "This is Poppy O'Hair over at the Tower Hair Salon. Could I order a hocus latte and… well, the other drink I usually order?"

"I'm new here. What other drink?" a girl asked.

Holly glanced over at Barry. He was drying a woman's hair with dragon flame. Not a good time to interrupt. "I'm not sure. How about you send one of everything?"

"Wow, you got it."

That should make Barry happy. But now she had to deal with Duchess. Holly went over her options. She could tell Duchess that she wasn't feeling well, and that they needed to reschedule. But this appointment was more than a haircut—it was Holly's opportunity to find out if Duchess had cursed the O'Hair sisters.

"I don't have all day!" Duchess called. "I'm due at the Red Shoes Studio in fifty minutes!"

"Sorry!" Holly grabbed Poppy's apron and hurried to her station. Duchess's black-and-white hair was pulled into a tight bun and decorated with a strand of pearls and some white swan feathers. Very carefully, Holly removed the adornments and pulled out the little pins that held the bun in place. Duchess's hair tumbled free. "Is something wrong?" Duchess asked snippily when she noticed that Holly was staring at her.

It had just occurred to Holly that if Duchess had cursed the O'Hairs, then Duchess would know that Holly was pretending to be Poppy. And if she knew, then why would she allow Holly to cut her hair? But if Duchess hadn't cursed the sisters, and if this was the work of fairytale magic, as Holly feared, then Duchess would have no clue.

"Should something be wrong?" Holly asked.

"I asked you first."

"Nothing is wrong with me." Holly had no idea what to think at this point. So she took a deep breath, then smiled. "Everything's great! Let's wash your hair." Duchess moved to the washing station. As she lay back in the chair, Holly tucked all of Duchess's hair into the bowl. Then she turned on the water and began washing. She remembered her sister telling her that people often spill secrets while getting their hair done. "So, we've established that nothing is wrong with me. But how are you? I heard you were at a competition."

"I just got back from a dance competition in Fairyland. Those fairies thought they'd win because they'd added flight to their dance moves, but little did they know, I can change into a swan." She snickered. "But now I'm totally stressed out because I have a paper to write for General Villainy, an hexam to study for in Chemythstry, and a ballet recital this weekend."

"You sound very busy."

"Busy? My feathers are totally ruffled!" She opened one eye. "Hey, that shampoo smells different. I want you to use my regular shampoo."

"Of course," Holly said. She stared at the array of products. Fortunately, Barry had been watching from the other room. He pointed. She picked up a red bottle. He shook his head. She picked up a yellow bottle, then a white bottle. Finally, he nodded. She shampooed and rinsed. "So, Duchess, what kind of paper do you have to write in General Villainy? Is it about cursing people?" She wrapped a towel around Duchess's head.

"What do you care about papers? You told me you hate writing papers. Your sister's the one who likes to write."

"Yes, that's true, but I'm not in General Villainy, so I guess I'm curious. What are the rules about casting curses?"

"Curses are against the rules, unless it's an assignment. You curse someone, and you'll get hexpelled."

Duchess raised an eyebrow. "But there are some students who don't care. Some would cast curses if they got mad enough."

Was that a sign of guilt? Holly still wasn't sure. She began to comb through Duchess's hair. "So, how do you want your hair cut today?"

"How?" Duchess curled her upper lip in a sneer. "Why would I change? I want the same as always. The *usual*."

Holly was really starting to hate that word.

While Duchess read her magazine, Barry motioned Holly over to the equipment cart. He handed her a pair of shears. Then he whispered in her ear, "She likes it trimmed, perfectly straight, one inch off." He patted her arm. "Honey, I don't know what's going on with you, but I think you may need a vacation."

Never before had Holly wanted a vacation from her life, but it was starting to sound like a good idea.

Holly began to cut, slowly and carefully, leaning very close to Duchess's hair so she could get a better look. How difficult could this be? Just a little snip here, a little snip there. Duchess didn't flinch or seem one bit worried. Clearly, that was evidence that she had no idea that Holly was pretending to be Poppy. But, to make double sure, she needed to ask one more question. "So, Duchess, is there anything else that's stressing you out, besides thronework?"

"Why do you ask?"

"Well, I saw your comment on Holly's blog."

"Ugh. Don't remind me. That story was terrible! Making fun of my destiny is so rude. Swans are graceful, magnificent creatures while mice are furry vermin." Duchess shifted, and as she did, Holly's shears cut at an angle. Oops. "I don't know how you deal with your sister. I'm so sick of these perfect princesses with their perfect Happily Ever Afters. They really ruffle my feathers!" Duchess shifted again. Another oops with the scissors. Maybe Duchess wouldn't notice since she often wore her hair in a bun.

"I'm sure my sister wasn't trying to insult you," Holly said. "She'd never do that. But you seem really mad. Like how mad? Like *revenge* mad?"

Duchess snorted, but it sounded like a honk. "Revenge? I wish. But I'm too busy for revenge."

Holly should have been relieved. But she wasn't. She was *hugely* disappointed. If Duchess had cursed the sisters, then they could have gone to Baba Yaga for help, and Duchess would have been forced to uncurse them and everything would have returned to normal. So did this mean that something bigger, something more powerful was at work, trying to force Holly and Poppy to accept their birth order? Poppy was not going to like this discovery.

The haircut wasn't a total hack job. Most of it looked okay, except for a few uneven sections in the back.

Holly found the Cloud in a Box. She opened one of the packets. A tiny cloud emerged and floated over Duchess's head. "It's the latest," Holly explained. "It will give you a lovely natural look." Duchess seemed agreeable. While the cloud puffed up and blew a gentle breeze, and while Duchess thumbed through an issue of *Castle and Garden*, Holly hurried to the reception desk to check her phone in private. No hexts from Poppy. So she hexted:

**Sparrow's aunt wants sketches. Duchess didn't curse us.**

"Help!"

Holly ran back to the styling room. The puffy little cloud had turned gray and stormy. Lightning bolts were shooting out of it.

Duchess's hair was frazzled. She jumped out of the chair, her eyes blazing. "Oh feather dusters! Look what you've done to my hair!"

"I'm royally sorry," Holly said as she tried to catch the cloud so it couldn't do more damage.

Duchess grabbed her stuff. "Your sister is a royal pain, but I thought you were different. So that's why you were asking about revenge. You wanted to get me back for criticizing your sister's stupid story. Well, I have news for you, Poppy O'Hair—two can play at this game!"

As Duchess stomped out the door, five baristas entered, carrying trays loaded with coffee drinks—seventy total. "Order for Poppy O'Hair."

The cloud unleashed another lightning bolt and set one of the coffee cups on fire. Barry put a hand on Holly's shoulder. "Oh, honey, I think you'd better take the rest of the day off."

# Ruined

# Reputation

*N*ews traveled fast at Ever After High, like pixie dust in a windstorm.

By the time Holly had walked back to campus, everyone already knew what had happened at the salon. Holly ascertained this unfortunate fact from the way everyone was looking at her, pointing at her, and whispering.

*Uh-oh*, she thought.

Just as she made her way toward the dormitory, the quad's giant mirror screen lit up and a promo for

Blondie Lockes's news show, *Just Right*, began to play.

"Listen up, fairytales," Blondie's voice said. "Be sure to watch tonight's episode of *Just Right* to get the latest scoop on the Duchess Swan hair disaster." And then the headline *Fried Swan* appeared on the screen.

Holly cringed. Blondie had made it sound way worse than it was. She cringed again as she spotted Blondie hurrying toward her, curls bouncing with each eager footstep. "Poppy!" Blondie called. Holly tried to make her escape, but the intrepid reporter was way too fast. "Do you have any comments for my viewers?"

Holly frowned at the MirrorPad as it was shoved in her face. "Yes, I do have something to say. Duchess didn't get *fried*. That's a bit of an exaggeration. It was an accident. The Cloud in a Box didn't work right."

Blondie pressed the pause button. "Oh, I know that," she said to Holly. "But my viewership is at an all-time high. And I'm not going to get a record number of viewers if my tagline is *Cloud in a Box Didn't Work Right*." She giggled. "*Fried Swan* is so much better."

Holly leaned close to Blondie. "Can't you just ignore this?"

"Ignore it?" Blondie gasped. "I'm a journalist. I can't ignore a story any more than a princess can ignore a pea."

Holly was about to use the "I thought we were friends" plea, when Poppy's MirrorPhone rang. It was Barry, from the salon. "Honey,'" he said. "Don't freak out, but I have some bad news."

"What?" Holly asked, even though she truly didn't want to know.

"Your clients are calling and canceling their appointments."

"Why? It was just one little—" She stopped midsentence. Blondie was standing close enough to hear. "Okay, thanks for telling me." She hung up. Was this really happening? Had one little mistake ruined her sister's reputation?

"I'd love to interview you," Blondie said, pressing the record button. "So, Poppy, can you explain to my viewers what happened at the salon? Duchess thinks you were seeking revenge. Were you?"

"What?" Holly spat out the word. "No. Of course not. I wouldn't do something like that."

"Are you sure? You and your sister are very close. And Duchess publicly criticized your sister's writing."

"Yes, she did, but I'd never…" At this point, a crowd of students had gathered around. "Look, I'm sure my sister can fix it." She felt as frazzled as Duchess's hair. "I mean, I'm sure I can fix it. If Duchess comes to the salon tomorrow, I'll make her hair look great again." Poppy would know what to do.

"No way!" Duchess Swan pushed her way through the crowd and stood in front of Holly, her arms tightly crossed. Her usually glossy black-and-white hair looked as dry as straw. Thin ribbons of smoke curled from a few ends that were still sizzling. "I'm not letting you get near my hair ever again!"

Holly was about to say she was sorry, but Blondie

was quicker. "Poppy, if this wasn't revenge, is this a sign that you've lost your touch?"

"Of course not," Holly said. "I'm still an excellent stylist."

"Really?" Duchess snorted. "If this is your best, then I'd hate to see your worst."

How could Holly convince Duchess and everyone else that Poppy was still an excellent stylist? "If only you'd let me fix it. Tomorrow."

Sparrow hurried into the quad. "Hey, Poppy!" he called. "My aunt just phoned. She wants those sketches as soon as possible. IT'S SKETCHING TIME!"

Holly pulled him aside. "Listen, I can't draw right now."

"Why?" He scratched his soul patch. "How come you're acting so weird today? I thought you wanted this real bad."

"I do, but…" Holly's heart began to pound.

"Then why can't you draw those sketches right now?"

"Because I can't draw!" she wanted to holler. "I'm an imposter! I don't design outfits and hairstyles! I write!"

The confession wanted to burst free. "Because... because..." A weight pressed down on Holly, as if her hair had suddenly grown back. But it hadn't. "Because..."

She knew, then and there, that fairytale magic had made its claim. It was clearly telling her that she wasn't worthy of being firstborn. "Look at you," it was saying. "You messed up your sister's life by taking away her firstborn status, and now you are messing up her reputation. You don't deserve to be Rapunzel's heir."

Tears stung Holly's eyes. "I can't do this!"

"Do what?" Sparrow asked.

"This!"

She turned away from Sparrow. Away from Blondie and the other students.

And she ran.

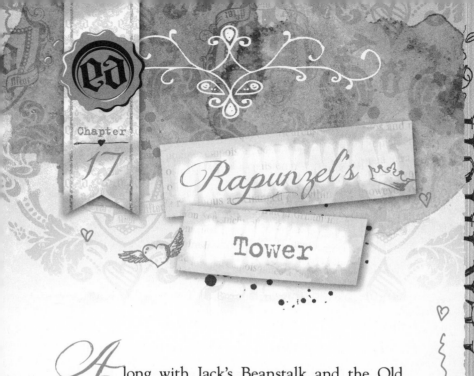

# Rapunzel's

# Tower

Along with Jack's Beanstalk and the Old Woman's Shoe, Rapunzel's Tower was one of the most popular tourist attractions in the fairytale kingdoms. No longer set in the Wild Wood, it had been carefully deconstructed, stone by stone, then rebuilt closer to town. This made it much easier for tourists, for no longer did they have to cut through deadly thickets, cross hydra-infested waters, or climb sheer cliffs that were slippery with bat guano in order to see Rapunzel's former place of imprisonment. Now they merely parked their chariots in the paved lot and walked the cobbled path to the ticket booth.

It was late afternoon when Holly stepped off the bus. She didn't want to talk to anyone, not even to her sister, so she'd turned off Poppy's MirrorPhone. She got in the long ticket line. No one paid special attention to her. Had she looked like herself, most would have recognized her as Rapunzel's daughter, but no one batted an eye. She didn't want the attention anyhow. She'd come there to think, to seek solace in a place that she'd held in reverence her entire life.

"Mom?" a little boy asked. "Why'd the lady live in this tower?"

"Because a wicked sorceress locked her inside," the mother said. They were standing a few places ahead in line.

"That's mean and rotten," the little boy said. "If a wicked sorceress tried to lock me in a tower, I'd fight!" He began beating a nearby bush with his plastic sword.

"She did fight," the mother said. "But she didn't

use a sword. She and the prince used their wits to outsmart the sorceress and escape."

*My mom used her wits. But how does one outwit fairytale magic?* Holly wondered. She stuck her hands into the pockets of her sweater tunic and waited as the line slowly moved forward.

The ticket taker was a troll with a bulbous nose the size of a pickled pear. "Price went up," he told her. "Tower needs a new roof." She paid the coin and took the little paper ticket. "If ya wanna wait, there's gonna be a tour in a half hour." He pointed to a group of tourists who were gathering under a tree. "Otherwise, ya can take one of these." He held up a tablet and a set of earphones. "It's got a voice on it that tells ya what yer looking at."

"No thanks," she said. She'd been there countless times. Besides, she'd written the audio tour, so she practically knew it by heart!

"What about a map?" the troll asked. He was a rather beefy fellow, even for troll standards.

"I know where I'm going. But thanks anyway."

"Suit yerself."

The tower door was a recent addition so tourists wouldn't have to climb through the only window, as the prince had years ago. The most famous saying from Rapunzel's story was etched in stone, above this new entry:

Rapunzel, Rapunzel, let down your hair.

Holly stepped through the entry and into the tower museum, which took up the entire ground floor. The circular room was filled with glass cases, each displaying an artifact from the story. One held the prince's leather boots, which he'd removed before his climb. Another held the sorceress's spectacles, which she'd dropped while chasing after Rapunzel and the prince. But the case that drew everyone's attention sat smack-dab in the center of the room. "Wow, what's that?" the little boy asked.

"That is Rapunzel's braid," his mother replied.

A sign below the case read:

> FUN FACT: RAPUNZEL'S BRAID MEASURES
> SEVENTY-TWO FEET LONG AND TAKES
> THIRTY BOTTLES OF SHAMPOO TO WASH.

Holly stood quietly to the side. No matter how many times she visited, the sight of the braid always amazed her and filled her with pride. But on this visit her heart felt heavy. She'd come to say good-bye to this legacy of hers, this *false* legacy. She wasn't meant to be the heir. She couldn't deny her birth order any longer. The proof was on her head.

She watched the faces of the tourists as they looked at the braid. A girl and her father entered. The girl pressed her face to the glass. "So, is this it?" she asked. "Is this the reason Rapunzel's famous? She grew a lot of hair?"

"I guess so," her dad said with a shrug.

"And her daughter has to do the same thing? That doesn't seem fair."

"Well, she doesn't *have* to do the same thing," the dad whispered. "Not unless she wants to. It's up to her."

Holly shook her head. They had no idea what they were talking about. They didn't know the power of fairytale magic. It didn't ask one's opinion or offer choices.

She headed up the stone staircase at the back of the museum. It was a tight squeeze as tourists walked in both directions. Holly slipped past an elderly couple who'd stopped to catch their breath. Then she entered Rapunzel's Room. The round room was small, with only one window. In the old location, it had offered a view of the Wild Wood's canopy, which had stretched all the way to the horizon. But now it looked down on the parking lot and a Henny Penny's Diner. The room contained a cot, mattress, blanket, and a brass wall hook where Rapunzel had secured her braid before letting it down. A shelf held a few items. There were reproductions of journals in which Rapunzel had recorded her inner-most thoughts and dreams—the originals were in

Rapunzel's possession. And there were stacks of books, the main source of entertainment during the long months of imprisonment. A small nest in the corner had once been home to her squirrel friends, who'd carried the books through the Wild Wood, thus enabling Rapunzel to prepare for her law degree. Rapunzel had read each and every book the squirrels had brought, even the squirrel-oriented ones on nut gathering and forest foraging.

In the courtyard below, the tour guide's voice bellowed. "Gather 'round for the last tour of the day!" Holly leaned against the wall and looked out the window. The tour guide stood on a bench, tourists crowded around her. "Once Upon a Time, in a faraway kingdom, a king and queen were preparing for the birth of their firstborn daughter."

Firstborn daughter. Holly's heart pounded. The ground raced up at her, so she stepped away from the window and closed her eyes. Her fear of heights was just another sign that she wasn't destined for the heir's role. *I've been so foolish*, she told herself.

Screams of glee arose outside. "It's Holly!" a few girls cried.

Despite the inevitable dizziness, Holly looked out the window again. A girl with ankle-length auburn hair was walking up the path. "Mom, look, it's Holly O'Hair!" Some ran forward for autographs. Those who'd been inside the tower raced outside to see. Poppy smiled and waved to the admirers. Was she enjoying the attention? She'd never wanted this role, but after spending a day as the heir, maybe she was starting to like it. Poppy walked past the ticket booth, then spoke to the tour guide.

"Ladies and gentlemen," the tour guide announced, "Ms. O'Hair wishes to have a few moments alone in the tower. We will wait out here until she is finished."

*Why did Poppy want to be alone in the tower?* Holly wondered. In the past, Poppy had never paid much attention to the tower. Though she'd visited with the family, she'd spent most of the time outside, climbing the trees, which made sense because towers weren't in her future. But had everything changed?

Did she want time alone because she'd enjoyed spending the day as the heir? Was the tower suddenly important to her? Holly's twintuition should have known the answer, but with all the subterfuge, she felt more confused than ever.

The sound of hurried footsteps grew louder and louder, until Poppy burst into the little room. "I knew I'd find you here!" Poppy exclaimed with a huge smile.

"You came here to find me?" Holly asked.

"Yes, of course. Why else would I come here?" She put her hands on her hips and narrowed her eyes. "Are you trying to hide from me or from the rest of the world?"

"All of the above." Holly sank onto the little cot. "I made a complete mess of things."

"I know," Poppy said, but she didn't look angry. "I've never seen such a terrible haircut. Duchess is *fuming*. Literally." She started to laugh.

Holly scowled. "How can you laugh? I'm the worst sister ever after. I ruined your reputation."

"No you didn't. It's one botched haircut. Everybody messes up once in a while. I've already promised Duchess a whole year of free cuts. That calmed her down."

"But what about all the cancellations?"

Poppy plopped onto the cot next to Holly. "I'll call my clients and explain. I'll tell them that the Cloud in a Box was faulty and I'll never use it again. They'll understand."

This sounded good, but Holly wasn't convinced. "But you should be mad at me. I didn't know what to say to Sparrow's aunt, so I told her that the new look was going to be classic. I think she hated the idea."

"Classic?" Poppy half smiled. "What? Like little hats with feathers, and green tights?"

"Uh-huh," Holly said with a gulp.

Poppy's half smile turned into a full smile. "Leave it to your twintuition to know exactly what I'd been planning."

"What?" Holly couldn't believe it. "Seriously? You were going to go classic?"

"Well, I was still debating it. Sparrow hates tights, and I knew he'd freak out." She gave Holly a devilish look. "But I'm pretty sure that if you tell him he looks good in a pair of tights, he'd go for it." She wagged her eyebrows in a teasing way.

"You know that he has a crush on me?" Holly asked.

"Of course I know."

"But the other day in the salon when I mentioned his name, you blushed," Holly pointed out. "I thought that meant that *you* had a crush on him."

"What?" Poppy laughed again. "No way. Sparrow and I are just friends. If I blushed, it was probably just from the heat. That salon gets hot when the sun streams through."

"Really?" Holly gave her sister a big hug. "I'm so relieved." Then she released the hug and slumped her shoulders. "But I'm still a terrible sister. I've been selfish."

"How can you say that?" Poppy asked. "It's not easy pretending to be me, and you did your best.

And here you are, more worried about me than about the meeting with the editor from Simon and Pieman. That's the opposite of selfish."

Holly went quiet for a moment. Amid all the uproar, she hadn't thought about Simon and Pieman for the entire afternoon. But that realization didn't change anything. "I've been selfish because I took all the glory from you. I kept pretending to be the firstborn, instead of giving you the opportunity to claim what was rightfully yours. I saw you waving and smiling at the tourists outside. You were enjoying the fame, I could tell. And why wouldn't you? It's wonderful, and I've taken that away from you. I should have stepped aside and let you have what is yours."

"Whoa, hold on!" Poppy jumped to her feet. "Sure, I was smiling and waving, but that's because I was pretending to be you. I don't want the fame. And I hate being recognized everywhere I go. It's a royal pain. And this hair is making me nuts." She pushed it out of her face. "How many times do I

have to tell you that I don't want to be Rapunzel's heir?"

"We don't have a choice," Holly said. "Duchess didn't curse us. No one cursed us. We have to face the truth. Fairytale magic controls our destinies."

Poppy turned away for a moment. Holly expected there'd be another long argument, like the last time she'd brought up this subject, but when Poppy turned back, she simply said, "Okay. I guess it's over."

Holly couldn't believe it. "Over?" she asked. She'd been expecting her sister to put up more of a fight.

"Yep. The magic won. Guess we'd better get on with our new lives." Poppy started toward the door. "I'm hungry. Wanna get a slice of pizza before we head back to school?"

"Wait." Holly slowly rose from the cot. "You're giving up? Just like that? But you're usually the fighter. You're the one who tells me that we have to make our own choices."

"We're tangled in this together," Poppy said. "I can't do it on my own. It takes two. So, if you think we shouldn't fight the magic, then we won't."

It was so odd to see Poppy like this. Ready to give in. To admit defeat. Was the weight of the long hair taking a toll on her? "But—"

"Look, Holly, you said fairytale magic has made the choice for us. And if that's how you feel, then you'll go and tell the world that I'm the firstborn. And I'll stand beside you and support you. But I'm never going to be the next Rapunzel. And if I'm not going to be Rapunzel, and you're not going to be Rapunzel, then I guess there just won't be one." She paused, giving time for that weighty statement to settle. "But I still say it's not necessary for you to give up the destiny. So what if your hair is going to be short forever after? If you want to be Rapunzel, then be Rapunzel!"

Holly ran a hand over her head. "But how can I without the hair?"

Poppy leaned against the door frame. "Do you

really think that's what Mom's story is about? Hair? Only hair? Do you really think that's her legacy?"

Holly frowned. Was that a trick question?

Poppy looked deep into Holly's eyes. "Whatever after you decide to do, I'm in it with you. I'll see you outside." Her footsteps faded as she made her way down the staircase.

Holly's thoughts spun. Hair *was* her legacy. The long, flowing, magically growing kind of hair. That was the heart of Rapunzel's story. Wasn't it?

She began to pace. She imagined Professor Nimble perched on his stool in the Tall Tales classroom, a scarf wound around his skinny neck, his long fingers sticking out the holes in his knit gloves. "Writers," he would say, "please write an essay on the main theme in Rapunzel's story."

Holly's fingers twitched as if they held a quill. She imagined the blank page. As she continued pacing, she began to work her way toward an answer. Rapunzel is the hero, and every hero has a quest. For

Jack, the quest was to get something to eat for himself and his mother. For Red Riding Hood, the quest was to get safely to her grandmother's house. For Holly's mother, the quest was to grow her hair super long so that the prince could climb it and rescue her. So she could be free of the tower. Free from a place where she'd been unfairly imprisoned. Free from the evil sorceress.

The theme was freedom!

Rapunzel and the prince risked their lives during the escape. But they did it for the freedom to be who they wanted to be, to live where they wanted to live, and to love who they wanted to love.

Freedom.

"Poppy!" Holly cried as she ran down the stairs. Poppy was standing in the museum. Holly grabbed her sister by the shoulders. "I don't care if I have short hair for the rest of my life. I'm going to be the next Rapunzel because that's what I want! End of story!"

Poppy smiled. "Now that's the kind of ending I like."

# A Mother's Twintuition

uring the bus ride home, Poppy signed a few more autographs. "Why not?" she whispered to Holly. "It's my last night pretending to be you. Thank goodness." She snickered. Then, after untangling her hair from a kid's backpack, she settled onto the seat next to Holly. "So, if I'm gonna be stuck with long hair for the rest of my life, what do you think about curls? I could get a perm."

"I can see you pulling that off," Holly said.

"Braids could also be nice. That would keep the hair out of my eyes while I'm working at the salon."

"I think braids would suit you."

Poppy nudged Holly with her elbow. "Aren't you dying to know about the meeting in Camelot?"

"Yes, please tell me." Holly anxiously gripped the armrest.

"Well, it was certainly easier than your day. I was worried that the editor was going to ask me all sorts of questions about your stories. But luckily, he just wanted to give me a tour of the publishing house. All I had to do was smile and nod. He said everyone at Simon and Pieman was very hexcited about the story collection and that *Tower Tales* should be out next spring."

"Wow." Holly relaxed against the seatback. A book. *Her* book. By next spring.

"You're supposed to go back in a few weeks so they can take a photo of you for the cover."

"They'll be a bit shocked by my new look," Holly

said. Then she shrugged. "But if they can't deal with it, they'll have to issue a complaint with fairytale magic." They both laughed.

It was dark when they got back to school. Had they arrived a few minutes later, it would have been impossible to sneak onto campus, thanks to the headmaster's magical wall of thorns, which protected the school's perimeter after curfew. Fortunately, the girls slipped in before the appointed hour, with only a minute to spare.

The campus lay in quiet slumber. Most students were in bed with lights out. An owl hooted from an alcove, and a few rats skittered between shadows. The girls tiptoed up the stairs to their tower room. It had been an exhausting day, and Holly was looking forward to tumbling into bed.

"Mother!" they both cried after opening their bedroom door.

Rapunzel sat on the edge of Holly's bed, with Clipper curled on her lap, purring, and with Barber tucked beneath a blanket, his nightcap in place. Her daughters ran to her and planted a kiss on each cheek. "What are you doing here?" Poppy asked.

Rapunzel looked at the daughter with the long auburn hair. "I'm here, *Poppy*, because it's time for you two to tell me what's going on."

"Wait, you know she's Poppy?" Holly asked.

"Of course I know." Rapunzel gently stroked the lion cub's head. "You've never been able to fool me."

"Never?"

"Well, I did get confused on the first day of your birth, obviously. When Nanny Nona put you in the wrong blanket, I didn't notice. But who could blame me? I was very tired. Giving birth to twins is not an easy feat."

"You know about the blanket mix-up?" Holly asked.

"I figured it out on your second birthday. I was going through old photos, and I noticed that the twin with the wild hair was in the wrong blanket." She pointed. The wild hair was as unruly as ever, even though it was now purple. "That hair is the only thing *wild* about you." She smiled sweetly at Holly.

"I don't understand," Holly said. She sat next to their mother. "If you knew the truth, why didn't you correct the mistake? Why didn't you tell me that I wasn't firstborn?"

Poppy pulled up a chair and sat across from them, eagerly awaiting the answer.

"I always thought it was odd that the more energetic of my children had been born second. So when I found that photo, it began to make sense." Rapunzel gently moved Clipper off her lap, then scooted closer to Holly. She took her hand. "Despite the fact that you are identical twins, by the age of two, you had developed very different personalities. You loved listening to fairytales, and you were very happy knowing that you'd grow up to live a fairytale life." She reached out and took Poppy's hand. "But you never showed any interest in those stories. You were running around, doing your own thing, clearly

a child with a mind of her own. You were a free spirit who wouldn't thrive within the constraints of prewritten destiny. I realized that the birth order didn't matter. You were both exactly who you were meant to be." She released their hands, then picked a tuft of lion cub fur from her skirt. "Unless, of course, you've changed your minds?"

"NO!" the girls cried.

"I'm glad to hear that."

Poppy's eyes widened. "So, you agree with me that we shouldn't tell anyone? Not even Father?"

"I do not like keeping secrets," Rapunzel said with a sigh. "Unfortunately, we live in a world where many still embrace the old royal traditions. Your father and his family believe very strongly, as does the headmaster of this school, in birth order and in the law that states that the firstborn inherits a parent's legacy. But I believe that's a ridiculous, out-of-date law. I will not allow it to stifle my daughters' dreams. It does not matter when you came into the world. What matters is what's in here." She pointed to her head. "And in here." She pointed to her heart. "So for now, I suggest that we don't mention our little secret to anyone."

That was the best news ever after! Holly and Poppy threw themselves at their mother and hugged her as ferociously as lion cubs.

"But what about fairytale magic?" Holly asked. "It's making Poppy's hair grow long and mine grow short."

"Fie on fairytale magic. If hair length is the only thing you have to worry about, then consider yourselves extremely fortunate." Then Rapunzel stood. "You know, Holly, I've been thinking. If you don't want to sit in your tower waiting to be rescued, I could help you turn it into a writing studio."

Best. Idea. Ever. After!

# *Fairytale*

# Ending

*W*hat happened the next morning was the stuff of fairytales. And since life *is* a tale, one that is lived instead of told, it all made perfect sense to Holly.

When she opened her eyes, she realized that she'd slept better than she had since learning the truth about her birth order. It had been the kind of sleep that was so deep and peaceful, she couldn't remember any dreams or any stirrings. Her body and her mind felt at ease. She stretched, yawned, then gently moved her snoring lion cub so she could get out of bed.

When she pushed back the covers and sat up straight, she found herself swimming in a sea of long auburn hair. It cascaded down her shoulders and back, a comforting sensation, like a hug. "Poppy," she whispered. Barber was already sitting on the windowsill, waiting to be let out. Holly opened the window. The monkey grabbed a vine and climbed down the wall. Then he scampered toward the woods. There was no need to imprison him in a tower. He needed the trees. He needed his freedom. "Poppy," Holly repeated.

Poppy bolted upright and blinked in wonderment at her sister. "Your hair is back," Poppy said. She threw back the covers. "Then that means…" Poppy rushed to the vanity and grabbed her shears. Her hair still reached to the floor, but this time when she cut it, it did not grow back. "Oh thank the godmothers!" she exclaimed as the cut locks fell to the carpet. "I'm myself again!"

While Poppy cut and dyed her hair, Holly had just enough time to write her essay for Tall Tales. The words flowed, without hesitation. Over the last few days, she'd formed a definite opinion about fate. Or fairytale magic, as she liked to call it. She couldn't wait to share it with the class.

"Why do you think we got our hair back?" Poppy asked once she was dressed in her sweater tunic and leggings.

"In every hero's quest, there is a test," Holly said as she stuffed her notebook and quill into her book bag. "We passed ours."

Poppy thought for a moment. "We chose to be our true selves," she said. Holly nodded. Poppy grabbed her jacket, and they headed down the stairs. "You know, even though yesterday was a pretty crazy day, I think that curse was the best thing that ever happened to us."

"I couldn't agree more."

"Hey, Poppy!" Sparrow hurried across the quad, his

guitar hanging against his back. "You feeling better today?"

Poppy looked at him with confusion. "What do you mean?"

"You were totally weird yesterday."

Poppy glanced at Holly. "Oh yeah, that. Well, I'm definitely feeling better."

Then Sparrow grinned at Holly in a goofy sort of way. "Hi, Princess."

"Hi, Sparrow," she said.

"Wanna hear my new song? It's about you." He swung his guitar around and was about to play an eardrum-shattering chord, when Poppy reached out her hand and placed it over the strings.

"Sparrow," she said kindly, "we don't have time right now. We need to get those sketches to your aunt, remember?" She patted her book bag.

"Oh right." He pushed his shaggy bangs from his eyes. "You sure you want to do this whole classic thing with the tights? Don't you think we should

look a little more ROCK AND ROLL?" A pair of birds squawked as Sparrow sang those last three words. A wolf howled in the distance.

Holly stepped forward. "Sparrow, I think the whole retro thing will be cool. And my sister's the best stylist in this kingdom. You can trust her. She'll make you guys look spelltacular."

"You think it will be cool?" Sparrow's doubts visibly melted away. "Awesome! Then I guess everyone better get ready, cause we're bringing back CLASSIC HOOD." He and Poppy started walking away, but he turned back and hollered, "Hey, Princess, I almost forgot, your sister said you'd go out with me sometime."

Poppy was about to disagree with this statement, but Holly winked at her. After all, Holly had put herself into this situation. While she didn't feel *that* way about Sparrow, she'd come to realize that he wasn't so bad. "Sure, we can get together," Holly said, "but let's not think of it as a date." Sparrow furrowed his brow, obviously disappointed. "Let's

think of it as a way to collaborate. You're a writer, I'm a writer. How about you create a song to go along with one of my stories?"

"Whoa!" he said. "You just blew my mind. I'm all over that idea!" Then he and Poppy headed for the tree house.

Holly turned and was about to make her way to the classroom, when a tall figure stepped in front of her. Headmaster Grimm, standing in his usual commanding way, peered down at her. "Ms. O'Hair, do you have a moment?"

"Of course, Headmaster." Holly shifted the weight of her book bag. What was this about? Was he going to ask her why she hadn't terminated her blog? She squared her shoulders, ready to defend herself.

"It has come to my attention that you have received a publishing offer from a distinguished company in Camelot."

"Yes. Simon and Pieman."

"I see." He raised a bushy eyebrow. Holly shuffled in place. She couldn't tell if his expression was one of disappointment or approval. He stared at her as if he'd never seen her before.

"My stories," she explained. "The ones from my *Fairytale Fangirl* blog. They are going to put twelve of them into a book. So you see..." She swallowed hard. "I want to keep my blog. I want to keep writing my stories." She waited for what was sure to be a long lecture.

He raised his other eyebrow. Then he smiled. "Of course you should keep writing your stories. It bodes well for our institution that we've produced a published author, and one so young. I expect that in your book, you will acknowledge the school's role in encouraging you down this successful path."

Holly held back a gasp. Talk about changing one's tune! "Yes, of course, Headmaster."

He reached out, patted her head as if she were one of his cubs, then strode away.

By the time Holly got to the Tall Tales classroom, everyone was taking their seats. Professor Nimble was perched, as usual, on his stool. "Hello, writers," he said in his unusually high voice. "I'm quite eager to hear your essays. Who would like to go first?"

Holly's hand shot into the air, as if it had a mind of its own. The professor motioned her forward. She grabbed her essay and stepped to the front of the class. She looked out at familiar faces. Creative students, like herself, who cherished the role stories had played in their lives. And who wanted to be a part of making new stories. New adventures. New voices.

Holly pushed her long hair behind her shoulders. Then she clutched her paper and cleared her throat. And she read the first line of her essay.

"Fate will not write my story. I'm here to write it myself."

# About the Author

Suzanne Selfors feels like a Royal on some days and a Rebel on others. She's written many books for kids, including the Smells Like Dog series and the Imaginary Veterinary series.

She has two charming children and lives in a magical island kingdom, where she hopes it is her destiny to write stories forever after.

$\mathcal{C}$an't get enough Ever After High?
Keep reading about your
best friends forever after in
**The School Story collection**
by Suzanne Selfors: